THE HAUNTED VIOLIN

TRUE NEW ENGLAND GHOST STORIES

Rock Village Publishing
41 Walnut Street
Middleborough MA 02346
(508) 946-4738

Other books by Edward Lodi

Deep Meadow Bog:
Memoirs of a Cape Cod Childhood

Cranberry Chronicles:
A Book About A Bog

Forty-one Walnut Street:
A Journal of the Seasons

Cranberry Gothic:
Tales of Horror, Fantasy, and the Macabre

Shapes That Haunt New England:
The Collected Ghost Stories of Edward Lodi

Haunters of the Dusk:
A Gathering of New England Ghosts

The Haunted Pram:
And Other True New England Ghost Stories

Murder on the Bogs:
And Other Tales of Mystery and Suspense

Ida, the Gift-Wrapping Clydesdale:
A Book of Humorous Verse

The Ghost in the Gazebo:
An Anthology of New England Ghost Stories
(editor)

Witches of Plymouth County:
And Other New England Sorceries

Witches and Widdershins:
A Modern-day Witch Story

The Old, Peculiar House:
Ghost Stories Read by the Author
(one-hour audio on CD)

THE HAUNTED VIOLIN
TRUE NEW ENGLAND GHOST STORIES

ROCK VILLAGE PUBLISHING
MIDDLEBOROUGH, MASSACHUSETTS
First Printing

The Haunted Violin
Copyright © 2005 by Edward Lodi

"The Hauntings of Pachaug Forest"
Copyright © by David Trifilo

Typography and cover by Ruth Brown

Grand Manan photographs
courtesy of the Pennypackers

All rights reserved. No part of this book may be reproduced or
transmitted in any form, electronic or mechanical,
without written permission from the author,
with the exception of brief excerpts for review purposes.

ISBN 0-9721389-8-6

Dedication

To the Get-together Crew
You know who you are!

...should you not believe in, approve of, or enjoy the tales, just mark the small price of this little volume off as a loss. If you do not have the imagination, sympathy, or feeling for the supernatural to believe in these experiences of your fellowmen and derive some little pleasure from them, I am sure that you have suffered many losses much greater than this one.
—*Julian Stevenson Bolick,* THE RETURN OF THE GRAY MAN

Contents

- 1   Joe Baker Stops By
- 5   Postscript to "Joe Baker"
- 11   The Old Man of Grand Manan
- 23   And Yet Another Old Man
- 31   Play It Again, Harold
- 39   Hard-Hearted Hannah
- 41   At the Keyhole of Eternity
- 47   King Philip's Head
- 51   The Tortured Tree
- 55   The Bogman's Tale
- 61   The Ghost of Brunswick High
- 63   The Man in the Three-Cornered Hat
- 69   Tales and Ales
- 73   The Haunted Library
- 83   *The Hauntings of Pachaug Forest (by **David Trifilo**)*
  - 85   *Introduction*
  - 87   *Mrs. Gorton's Lilacs*
  - 91   *The Breakneck Hill Guard*
  - 93   *The Cries of the Indian Woman*
  - 95   *The Lantern & The Pipe*
- 99   *From the Archives*
  - 101   *The Dead Ship of Harpswell*
  - 103   *Jack Welch's Death Light*
  - 105   *The Owl Tree*
- 109   *Sources and Books Mentioned in the Text*

Joe Baker Stops By

This story was told to me on more than one occasion, and in more than one version, back in the 1960's, when I was a student at Boston University and worked part-time for the Tweedy and Barnes Cranberry Company in Wareham. In the various renditions the names of the principals varied; I've compromised and supplied names of my own making.

"Joe Baker Stops By" won first prize in the "Strange Occurrences" contest sponsored by Prime Time Cape Cod *and was published in the May 2003 issue.*

On frost nights, during the spring and fall seasons, many of the local cranberry growers—the bog owners themselves or their trusted foremen—would gather at Sam Pearce's screen house. The ramshackle building, though set deep in the woods off a dirt road at the edge of a swamp, was more or less centrally located. It offered the men a place where they could sip coffee (or maybe something a bit stronger) and while away a portion of the long hours in front of a cozy wood stove in the company of fellow human beings.

Sometimes they stayed for only a few minutes, sometimes for an hour or two—depending on the urgency of the frost warning, and the location of the bogs for which they were responsible. The more fortunate growers had electricity at their disposal; as soon as the temperature dipped to a crucial level they had only to flip a switch and set the pumps working. Others had to deal with gasoline or bottled gas and the vagaries of engines that might, or might not, start.

All had to periodically check their thermometers, which were tucked here and there among the cranberry vines or along the dikes, near ditches and reservoirs in dark, unlighted places, far from the nearest habitation.

It was dangerous work. Muskrats undermined the dikes; it was not uncommon for a man to sink through loosened turf and twist his ankle or break a leg. A shovel or rake or other tool carelessly tossed on the ground in the light of day could in the pitch black of night lead to a fall and serious injury. Trash racks—the metal grating that trapped debris from rivers and reservoirs and prevented it from clogging pump shafts or pipelines —needed periodic cleaning. A false step could send a man plunging down a steep embankment, or into the shaft itself.

Something of the sort happened to a cranberry grower named Joe Baker back in the 1950's, they say. As Jack Perry recalled (years afterward), it was just shy of midnight one Saturday toward the end of May, when the latch to the screen house door lifted and Joe came trudging in.

"Nothing unusual in that, of course, 'cept he was dripping wet. Looked like he'd gone for a swim with all his clothes on. His boots squished as he crossed the floor, I remember that."

Sam Pearce was there: "A handful of fellows was gathered around the stove, half dozing or quietly chatting away. It was the third straight night that week we'd stayed out for frost and everybody was dog tired."

Other than a polite nod, no one said anything to Joe when he entered the room. "He wasn't the sort of fellow you joked with," Bill Harju—who was also there that night—told me. "He wasn't mean or anything. Just the kind of guy who liked to be given a wide berth. He minded his business and you minded yours. If he'd taken a tumble, why, so had we all, some time or other. Sam and me exchanged glances but didn't say nothing."

"Keep in mind the only lighting in the room was from a smelly kerosene lantern Sam kept in one corner," Jack Perry explained, when he related his version of the story. "You couldn't make out the expression on Joe's face, to tell whether he was mad with hisself or not for being so clumsy, but like I said, you could hear his boots squishing as he walked up to the stove to dry hisself off. He stood in front of the stove for a couple minutes then pulled up a chair behind it, in the shadows.

"That's about all that happened, 'cept five minutes later Bob Kelley bursts onto the scene and says, all excited, 'I just found Joe Baker dead! Found him floating in the canal to his pump house.' Bob's bog was next to Joe's, you see, and they usually stopped by one another's on frost nights.

"'Don't be a damn fool. Joe Baker is setting right there behind you,' Sam said, and we all glanced over to the corner where we'd seen him plunk hisself down, just five minutes before, but there wasn't nobody there, just a wet impression on the wooden chair, and a puddle of dirty water on the floor."◊

Postscript to "Joe Baker"

Full fathom five thy father lies;
Of his bones are coral made;
Those are pearls that were his eyes.
Nothing of him that doth fade
But doth suffer a sea-change
Into something rich and strange.
   —William Shakespeare, The Tempest

A true ghost story—with a Cape Cod setting—that bears a slight resemblance to "Joe Baker Stops By" was published as long ago as 1934. It was told to the New York drama and literary critic and essayist, Alexander Woollcott, who included it in his collection of essays, *While Rome Burns*.

Woollcott cut quite a figure in his day. He wrote regularly for *The New Yorker* magazine, and for many years had his own radio show. Moss Hart and George Kaufman went so far as to write a play based on him: *The Man Who Came to Dinner*. In the theatrical version the accomplished Woollcott appeared in the leading role. In 1941 the play was made into a movie; Monty Woolley starred, along with Bette Davis, Ann Sheridan, and Jimmy Durante. According to many critics, *The*

Man Who Came to Dinner was the greatest role of Woolley's career.

(Woollcott. Woolley. The similarity of the names is pure coincidence, I suppose. As is the fact that Woollcott died in 1943, the year in which I was born. But then, there are those who claim there are *no* coincidences.)

Woollcott titled his story "Full Fathom Five," undoubtedly from the well-known quotation from Shakespeare's last play, *The Tempest*. The story was told to him by a friend, Alice Duer Miller, who had heard it years earlier from Mrs. George Haven Putnam, dean of Barnard College. Interestingly enough, after Woollcott had already written and published the story he learned additional details, from none other than the Curator of the Botanical Museum in St. Louis. I mention all this to demonstrate the reliability of his sources.

Anyhow...

One evening in late October—it may have been Halloween itself—two sisters were driving along a lonely road in the vicinity of Woods Hole. This was in the early days of automobiles, prior to 1910, when both "horseless carriages" and the roads they traveled on were primitive. As frequently happened in those days, the car the sisters were driving broke down and they found themselves stranded, with little hope of another car coming by to offer assistance until the following day.

There were no street lamps of course; the only light to see by was that cast by the moon. And the only habitation in view was an apparently abandoned house set well back from the road, partially concealed by trees and hidden in shadows.

A bone-chilling wind blowing off the Atlantic convinced the sisters to seek shelter. Although they didn't much care for the looks of the old house, it seemed preferable to the exposed automobile, so grabbing the blankets that all prudent travelers carried with them in those early days of motoring, they crossed the long-neglected lawn to the front door.

Even though they were certain the house must have been vacant for years, they felt obligated to pull the bell cord, and receiving no response, to knock loudly on the door panel. The only answer to their knocking was the flapping, in the brisk wind, of a loose shutter on one of the windows.

When they investigated, they found the window to be unlocked; peering through the dusty panes they saw, with the aid of flashlights, that the room within had once been the library. A handful of books remained on the shelves and pieces of broken furniture lay scattered about. A thick layer of dust covered everything, including the bare floor. The brick fireplace that occupied the center of one of the outer walls remained cold and empty.

Convinced that the house had stood tenantless for a number of years, the sisters felt no compunctions about entering through the unlatched window and stretching out their blankets on the floor to spend the night.

Eventually, despite the drab surroundings and the many strange sounds indigenous to an abandoned house, the two women drifted off to sleep—only to be awakened suddenly and simultaneously by a sensation they could not identify: a sixth sense perhaps, or merely the feeling that they were no longer alone. Terrified, they opened their eyes to see that a man had entered the room. He was dressed as a sailor and stood dripping wet in front of the cold fireplace, as if attempting to dry himself by a nonexistent fire. Almost immediately the sisters realized that it was no living man they saw, but rather a ghost, a wraith no more substantial than the mist he seemed composed of.

One of the sisters involuntarily let out a scream and the ghost, uttering a moan, vanished into thin air, as if he had never existed. And that is what the two women tried to convince themselves: that there had been no one there, that what they thought they saw was nothing more than a bad dream, or at most the play of moonlight and shadows against the cold fireplace. Somehow they managed to fall back to sleep, and slept until wakened by the morning sun.

As they rose stiff and sore from a night spent on the hard floor, their gaze fell on a puddle of water lying in front of the fireplace where the ghostly sailor had stood. All else around the puddle was dry, the dust unmarked, showing no footprints or other signs of disturbance. When they investigated, they found that the shallow pool of water contained a small piece of green seaweed. One of the sisters scooped it up and wrapping it in a cloth carefully put it away for future reference.

Later that morning, after having sat in their car and been rescued by a kind passerby, the sisters ate breakfast in a local tavern while repairs were being made. They asked the tavern keeper if she knew anything about the old house on the lonely road in which they had spent the night.

"Oh, that place has been empty for nearly twenty years," their hostess told them. "It's supposedly haunted, if you put stock into that sort of thing. Some story about a fight between father and son, and the son running away, and later being drowned at sea. They say the family had to move out because of strange goings on. Weird things that happened, or were seen, during the night."

Sometime later the sisters were at a party in New York, where they met the curator of a museum. Hearing their story of the haunted house on Cape Cod, the curator asked to see the piece of seaweed, if they still had it. They did indeed have the seaweed, having preserved it by drying it in the sun, and they gladly passed it on to him for examination.

His report? Why, that the seaweed was a rare variety which grew only in deep waters, off the coast of Australia.

✧✧✧

Footnote

Louis C. Jones included a version of the above story in *Things That Go Bump in the Night: Haunted Trails & Ghostly Tales* (published in 1959). Although he makes reference to both Alexander Woollcott and Bennett Cerf (who reported hearing a similar tale), the version that Jones heard takes place during World War II. He heard it "on a day coach of the New York Central from a woman who happened to sit next to [him] from Syracuse to Lyons. She assured [him] that the circumstances were perfectly true." As is frequently the case with classic folk tales (i.e., urban legends), the woman telling the story claimed to have heard it from friends who personally knew the people involved.

In the World War II rendition, a woman whose husband is a naval officer fighting somewhere in the Pacific hears a noise issuing from her child's bedroom. She goes to investigate and sees her husband, in his uniform, looking at the child. When she speaks he vanishes, leaving a pool of water near the crib where he stood. She investigates and finds a piece of seaweed floating in the water. She scoops up the seaweed and takes it to an acquaintance, a marine botanist who teaches at a local university. After careful examination, the botanist identifies the seaweed as a rare type found in the South Pacific—a type that "grows only on the bodies of the dead."◊

The Old Man of Grand Manan

We have silent ghosts, and ghosts that lift your scalp with eerie rising screams. We have invisible ghosts, and ghosts that appear as pirates wearing silver buckles, or, a favorite posture, with their heads tucked under their arms; or manifest themselves merely as dancing lights or flickering masses of flame at sea. Our fraternity of famous ghosts, with an encouraging absence of discrimination, includes equal numbers of Englishmen and Frenchmen and Indians, but especially young lovers. We even have a haunted mountain, and an island that became a ghost.
  —Stuart Trueman, An Intimate History of New Brunswick

◊◊◊

Let us go and cool off at Grand Manan. I spent two months there some summers ago, fishing and dredging, and can assure you that it is the finest place on our whole coast...The scenery is superb. Huge, rocky cliffs, a thousand feet high, rise right out of the water, and are broken into the wildest and most romantic caves and inlets.
—Robert Carter, A Summer Cruise on the Coast of New England, *1858*

◊◊◊

Grand Manan is an old world island where courtesy and character are important and people value friendship most of all. Grand Manan is still natural.   —from a brochure describing the Marathon Inn

Grand Manan, New Brunswick, Canada, is definitely not a part of the United States of America, let alone New England. So what, you may reasonably ask, is a chapter which consists of ghost stories set on a Canadian island in the Bay of Fundy doing in a book about *New England* hauntings?

The answer is this: at one time in its turbulent history Grand Manan (pronounced Grand Muh-NAN) was claimed by Massachusetts (the part of Massachusetts that is now the state of Maine); moreover, some of the tales and legends included here date back to those early years. And the clincher: the most authentic, the most chilling, ghost story about Grand Manan begins on the mainland, in Machias, Maine.

◊◊◊

There is a legend on the island of a ghostly visitor to the village of North Head. This apparition comes in the guise of an old man, with a strange—but true—tale to relate: of lost lovers and bloodthirsty pirates.

In 1824, on the eve of their wedding day, two young lovers—Desilda St. Clair, renowned for her beauty and good grace; and Edmond Chatfield, equally handsome and well mannered—went rowing off the coast of Machias. As lovers will, they lost track of time until, abruptly, they found themselves caught up in a strong current that swiftly carried them away from the safety of shore and far out to sea. Though Edmond, ably assisted by his fiancée, frantically fought the current, he was unable to bring the boat back to shore; by nightfall the couple were hopelessly lost. To make matters worse, the wind blew a gale that drove them all the way to the cliffs of Grand Manan.

There their luck worsened. Daybreak found them wet and bedraggled. While huddling under what little shelter they could find and hoping for rescue, they fell into the hands of a band of pirates who had come to the island to bury treasure. The pirates brought the couple to Dark Harbour, where they chained Desilda to a tree and forced her to watch while they tortured and hanged Edmond.

When the picaroons had finished with Edmond they turned their attention to Desilda. They took turns raping her, all the while brutally beating her, until crazed by the ordeal she ran off into the woods, to the jeers of her drunken abductors. Though half insane, Desilda vowed vengeance, and somehow lured the pirates one by one into the woods, where she bashed in their heads with rocks. When the last pirate was dead, she ran shrieking up and down the shore until she, too, dropped dead from exhaustion.

This last scene was witnessed by a group of fishermen, who later passed on the tale.

As late as 1902 it was claimed, by more than one source, that in the wee hours of the bleakest nights the shape of a woman might be seen in the vicinity of North Head, crying out "Edmond! Edmond! Edmond!" Her ghostly phantom "sailed over fences, across Rodney Lane toward Whale Cove and over Fish Head." As for the unfortunate Edmond, even to this day he can sometimes be seen in foul weather, headless, racing along the shore.

Ferry at Black's Harbour

And the old man who, like the Ancient Mariner, appears from the shadows to repeat this tragic tale, only to vanish again into the gloom? No one can say for certain, but some believe he is the restless spirit of one of the fishermen who as a lad witnessed the final scene of bloodshed and horror, and who felt remorse all his life for not being able to come to the aid of the hapless Desilda.

◊◊◊

The comparison of the mournful blasts of a foghorn to the soulful sobbings of a ghost is a time-honored cliché, yet an apt one nonetheless, and on Grand Manan it is especially appropriate, for the island boasts a number of lighthouses and an even greater number of ghosts, some more vociferous than others.

In a region renowned for scenic beauty and picturesque lighthouses, Swallowtail Light stands out as one of the most prominent. Its beam is visible for miles; in periods of fog its horn is audible far out to sea. The Sunday in June when Yolanda and I arrived by ferry at the village of North Head began in sun but ended with heavy rain and dense fog. Our

Shallowtail Light

room in the historic Marathon Inn—within walking distance of the lighthouse —overlooked the harbor and lay well within the range of the horn's soothing blasts.

I grew up on Cape Cod. As a child on foggy nights I liked to snuggle in bed with the covers pulled up to my chin and listen to the muffled sounds of the world at large, and to the colloquy of ships as they passed through the Cape Cod Canal. I owe, I think, a lifelong fascination with ghosts, hauntings, and all things dark and mysterious to the sonorous imprint of those mournful foghorns. That night in the ancient inn, with the rain lashing the windowpanes and the wind howling like a banshee (yes, another clichéd metaphor, and equally apropos) was like a journey home again, back to Cape Cod and the distant past.

(This I fear will be a chapter of digressions. Grand Manan, with its wild beauty and island remoteness, does that to you—makes your mind wander, away from the humdrum and mundane, to the mysterious and grandiose, and everything in between.)

Built in 1871, the Marathon Inn has been in operation continuously

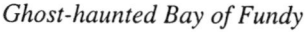

Ghost-haunted Bay of Fundy

since. It was established by James Pettes, a "retired" (at age 35) sea captain who appears to have been quite a character. But then, the inn's current owner, Jim Leslie, is also quite a character, in every positive sense of that word. An annex to the inn consists of a building erected in the early 1860's, which was moved from a place called Marble Ridge to its present location overlooking the harbour in 1898, when Captain Pettes won it in a poker game.

The inn proper, and to some extent the annex, have an old-fashioned, gothic feel to them. It might be an exaggeration to say that the Marathon Inn looks as though it had been drawn by the cartoonist Charles Addams—but not much of an exaggeration. Both buildings are warm and cozy and exude charm. And of course both are haunted.

Yolanda and I were staying at the Marathon Inn because of an Elderhostel. (No, I am *not* "the old man of Grand Manan" referred to in the title to this chapter. Despite the fact that I meet the age qualification for Elderhostel I'm not that old!) Jim sponsors more than a dozen Elderhostels each year. He acts as both host and tour guide, and occasionally as bartender and cook; on Friday for our final evening

Marathon Inn

meal at the inn he served up steaks and lobster, which he personally prepared to perfection.

Upon our arrival I immediately asked Cathy, the young woman behind the desk, whether there were any ghosts associated with the inn. "Oh yes," she replied. "There's the ghost of a woman who's been seen on the widow's walk. Ask Jim. He'll tell you all about it."

However, later that day when I did ask Jim his response was, in his typical deadpan manner: "There have been reports of ghosts. I've never seen one."

For the next several days despite my continued efforts to pry information from him he remained noncommittal. One morning as I happened to be leafing through a guidebook which Yolanda found lying on a coffee table called *Country Inns and Back Roads, North America*, I came upon a section labeled "MARATHON INN Grand Manan Island, 1976." It proved interesting reading, but one sentence I found especially intriguing: *On this particular trip Jim Leslie suggested in a very mysterious way that something unusual and exciting had been going on at the inn on at least two occasions during the year.*

Marathon Inn Annex

"Ah hah! Perhaps this entry contains the solution to the mystery surrounding the woman who haunts the widow's walk," I exclaimed to myself.

Alas. Further reading revealed that the mystery referred to involved, not ghosts, but rather a "murder whodunit," a Mystery Weekend in which guests participated in discovering clues and solving the culprit's identity.

In the course of the week I kept pressing Jim for ghost stories. Finally, Thursday evening as we sat chatting and sipping wine in the lounge he said, "I have one ghost story that I can tell you tonight. But tomorrow I'm going to tell you a *true* ghost story."

As it turned out, the story he related on Thursday was true in its own right. As I recall, this is the gist of it (though after two or three glasses of wine—or was it ale I was drinking that night?—I may have gotten one or two minor details wrong):

One night a woman named Doris, who was the assistant to Freeman Patterson, a well-known Canadian photographer, was staying alone in the annex. Though it contained two beds, her room lacked a desk or other convenient work space. Since she had to prepare for a slide show of Patterson's photographs for the following day, Doris used the spare bed on which to lay out the slides, which she carefully sorted and arranged before placing them in a box. When she finished she left the box in place on the bed. Before retiring for the night she locked the bedroom door from the inside and secured it with a dead bolt. (The windows to the room had been nailed permanently shut.)

She slept the night through.

When she awoke in the morning, though the door to the room was still securely locked and dead bolted, to her dismay she found the slides all in a jumble, some lying on the bed, some on the floor. More mysterious, a number of them lay scattered in the hallway, some even having been tossed outside on the parking lot. Many were never found.

Doris, a responsible, highly respected person, believed that something supernatural had occurred. Jim—who apparently does not put much stock in ghosts—offers an alternative theory. He speculates that Doris may have been sleepwalking. That in a sort of trance she unknowingly got up sometime during the night, overturned the box of slides, unlocked the door and the dead bolt, and carried handfuls of slides with her through the hallway and outside into the parking lot, all the while mindlessly littering them along the way.

Then, remaining in a deep trance, returned to her room and re-locked the door and the dead bolt, and crawled back into bed? Even Jim admits that this scenario is unlikely, but he can offer no other plausible explanation for what occurred.

Then again, there are those who maintain that the annex—formerly the Maple Ridge Inn—is definitely haunted, perhaps by the ghost of one of the three workmen who were accidentally killed when the building was moved after the infamous poker game, or perhaps by an itinerant ghost who may have moved along with the structure. He has been described as being dressed in a "funny" or "strange" way, "more like a French peasant than a turn-of-the-century English workman."

◇◇◇

If Jim doesn't actually believe in ghosts, what then of the *true* ghost story which he promised to tell? I'll get to that in a moment, but first I'd like to describe the bus which Jim uses to transport Elderhostlers and others around and about the island.

The bus is a 1979 "Blue bird," presumably a former school bus, which Jim has painted a bright blue. Even so, in places some of the original yellow shows through, giving it a jaundiced look. The cover to the battery compartment is missing, so that the battery is constantly exposed. For some reason known only to himself, Jim keeps the door to the bus open at all times—except when passengers are aboard—all through the night, and even in the pouring rain. Perhaps he does so because the bus reeks of gasoline fumes, especially after being fueled. I mention all this, not because the bus is haunted—though by rights it should be, given its rickety appearance and the fierce moanings and groanings it makes whenever Jim shifts gears or compels it to climb even the slightest incline—but rather to give insight into Jim's personality.

I have described his deadpan manner. With Jim, one can never be absolutely certain whether he is being serious or merely exercising his wry sense of humor.

When questioned about the 1979 "Blue bird" he says, "Before I bought this bus I used to drive an old bus." I thought he was being facetious, until Laurie Murison, the manager of the island's Whale and Seabird Research Station, and the naturalist who led a couple of our outdoor excursions, confirmed that what he said was true. According to Laurie the *old* bus had bad breaks. "Jim used to keep a rock in it for use as a chock to keep the bus from rolling. Sometimes the Elderhostelers had to get out and push."

Jim paid seven hundred dollars Canadian for his *new* bus—the 1979 "Blue bird"—though he believes he most likely could have got it for less.

❖❖❖

The Blue Bird

The Sunday of our arrival on the island was, as I mentioned, wet and dismal; that evening our Elderhostel orientation was held in the annex parlour in congenial surroundings, in front of a roaring fire. In contrast, the Friday of our "graduation" was mild and pleasant, too warm an evening for a fire. But Jim heated things up anyhow, with humorous accounts of previous goings on at the inn, including a *true* ghost story.

Let me begin by explaining that at the time of our visit Jim had been running the inn for approximately twenty-seven years. The events that he related that evening had taken place many years previous, in his callow youth. Let me also add that, though I tried my best to take accurate notes, Jim had all of us laughing so hard that, given my own uncontrolled mirth along with the deafening background noise, I cannot guarantee that all of the details of the following story are one hundred percent factual.

Anyhow, years ago Jim had working for him a man named John, as well as a handyman named Ambrose who lived on the property and kept chickens. Katie and Larry, a couple from New York City, were regular guests at the inn. One evening, for reasons that to me are still unclear, John convinced Jim that it might be fun to play a prank on Katie and Larry. When the couple were off visiting friends on the island John and Jim grabbed one of Ambrose's hens and carried it up to their room, number 17, and hid it in the closet. The unsuspecting pair returned later that evening and, after relaxing a bit, climbed into bed. Shortly thereafter they heard a strange *bwok*. (Jim does a perfect imitation of a hen which I cannot even come close to emulating; incidentally, he is an expert birder and can identify, by sight and sound, the many avian species on the island and can imitate many of their calls.) The *bwok* was soon followed by another. *Bwok. Bwok.* This continued for some time.

Being city folks, neither Katie nor Larry recognized the sound. During the night they got up several times and searched the room, without success. It wasn't until toward dawn that they finally located the source of the disturbance. "By that time," Jim says, "Larry's shoes were covered in shit."

After that it became a tradition, in ensuing years, for Jim to play an occasional prank on his two friends from New York. The culmination came when Jim, in possession of a tape of sound effects, placed two powerful speakers in the crawl space under Room A, the room in the annex in which Katie and Larry were staying. At two a.m. the floorboards of Room A reverberated with, among other amplified noises, dogs barking, a gate creaking, and the deafening roar of a jet plane.

It wasn't until about fifteen years later that Jim happened to be reading a book about New Brunswick hauntings and came upon a *true ghost story* that featured the Marathon Inn. It seems that one night, many years ago, a woman staying in the annex was awakened in the wee hours and terrified by strange, inexplicable sounds: dogs barking, a gate creaking, and the deafening roar of a jet plane.◊

And Yet Another Old Man

And the island that became a ghost? You can see it from Grand Manan in the Bay of Fundy—Inner Wood Island, a mile off shore. Settled many years ago because it was close to good fishing grounds, the island had a population of 120, including forty-one schoolchildren...Today, deserted and lifeless, it is an unworldly place to visit...Only the creaking of loose doors breaks the heavy silence.
—*Stuart Trueman,* An Intimate History of New Brunswick

◇◇◇

As the ship approaches the weathered wharf in North Head, you'll see the Marathon Inn up on the hill. This is a working harbour. The men in the boats earn their living from the sea. The docks, the houses on stilts, the sight, sound and clean smell of the ocean are yours for as long as you stay. —*from a brochure describing the Marathon Inn*

In the rich and varied history of Grand Manan, pirates—and their hidden treasure—are recurring themes.

In the village of North Head not too many years ago three fishermen discovered that they each had dreamt the same dream: of pirate gold buried in the sand under certain cliffs overlooking the Bay of Fundy. Agreeing that this shared vision was a portent not to be ignored, the three left off fishing for a day and, armed with spades and picks, set off for the spot they recognized in their mutual dream. As soon as they arrived on the fog-drenched shore they began to dig. But no sooner had the first pick broken ground when they heard the sounds of chains rattling, and the prow of a ghost ship appeared through the parting mists. On the bow stood a fearsome specter, a skeletal pirate brandishing a sword.

The terrified fishermen did not wait for the fleshless buccaneer to introduce himself but instead took to their heels, and never returned to the spot—not even to retrieve their tools, which in their panic they had flung to one side. Sometime later a fellow townsman found the discarded implements but wisely did not use them, nor any others, to dig for treasure which he knew to be so fiercely guarded.

Perhaps there are readers of this book who are not so easily deterred, and would like to try their luck at unearthing the hidden hoard. Grand Manan is within easy reach—only ninety minutes by ferry from Black's

The Hole in the Wall

Harbour, New Brunswick; and there may be islanders willing to point out the spot where the three fishermen began, and immediately abandoned, their quest. While on the island be sure to visit The Hole in the Wall, a natural rock formation which, besides being wondrous to behold, is said to be a portal through which spirits enter and leave this world. Should you be so bold as to disturb the guardians of the buried treasure, you yourself may wish to beat a hasty retreat.

    A man who—even though confronted by what could only be the ghost of a pirate—did not beat a hasty retreat, was warden Vernon Bagley of Grand Manan's Seal Cove. While guarding a bird sanctuary one day, Bagley happened to be looking through his binoculars when he spotted a strange man approaching. The man was strange not only because he was unknown to the warden, but also because he was dressed like a pirate—red bandanna, long coat and all—and wore a loose sword hanging from his belt. As he came closer Bagley saw that, even though he had just emerged from the ocean, he was completely dry. The stranger seemed to be in a trance, or at least unaware of the presence of another. When the warden hailed him he puffed up his cheeks and roared like a

Cliffs of Grand Manan

lion, but kept on walking until he disappeared into a narrow strip of woods. Though Bagley put after him, he was unable to locate the man, even with the help of a police officer who happened by in a cruiser.

In Bagley's own words: "He just vanished! And I've never seen him since…and I don't know as I want to."

The ghostly pirate has been seen at least one more time, though, by a couple of kids toasting hot-dogs on the beach. When they spotted the weird stranger approaching through the mist they became frightened, and one of them dropped a hot-dog into the fire. The stranger bent over, raked the red-hot coals with his bare hands, and seized the hot-dog. The kids didn't hang around to see what he did next but ran away in fright.

◇◇◇

The rattling of chains has long been associated with ghosts and is often a sign of their presence. There are practical reasons for this. Throughout history prisoners have been chained to walls in dungeons and left there to starve, or were tortured to death, and until fairly recent times criminals were hanged in chains and their bodies left to rot on the crossroads as a warning to passersby. It's only natural—or supernatural—that the restless spirits of those who died such nasty deaths should carry their fetters around with them. (The heavy chains are also symbolic of the weight of sins.)

Off the shores of Grand Manan, in periods of dense fog, fishermen claim that they sometimes hear across the placid waters the rattling of chains and frantic voices speaking in a strange language. They know full well whom it is they are hearing: the ghosts of Chinese laborers from the nineteenth century being smuggled onto the mainland to work on the railroads, who when British warships approached were chained together and deliberately thrown overboard by orders of their ship's captain, so as to destroy the evidence of his crime, punishable at the time by death by hanging.

Cheney was the captain's name, and *his* ghost, too, is said to haunt the area. Telephone linemen repairing lines on Cheney's Island were run off by an irate man dressed in a nineteenth-century sea captain's uniform. When the men returned to the mainland and reported the incident, their boss told them not to worry, it was only the ghost of old Captain Cheney acting peevish.

An old gent who acts—or acts out—in an entirely different manner can be found in Grand Manan's aptly named Ghost Hollow. Some dark, gloomy night when the fog's near as thick as pea soup, folks say, you'll be driving along the lonely stretch of road, when this crazy coot of a man wearing a black hat tilted at an outlandish angle on his head and a wild grin on his face comes dashing out of the woods and runs alongside your car, then suddenly spurts ahead and flings himself in front of the wheels. In a panic, you think you've struck him, but when you get out he's no longer there. As, bewildered, you climb back into the driver's seat a shrill peal of maniacal laughter rings out, so close to your ear you jump half out of your skin with fright.

A ghost who thinks he's a clown!

Perhaps he *is* a clown—a revenant from Grand Manan's own Circus of Horrors.

In the fall of 1836 a traveling circus with the cumbrous name of Dexter's Locomotive Museum and Burgess's Collection of Serpents and Birds toured up and down the coast of New Brunswick. At the end of the tour the circus departed for Portland, Maine, on the side-wheeler *Royal Tar*, a new steam ship under the command of Captain Thomas Reed. Besides the ship's crew, the vessel carried sixty-one men and women associated with the circus and thirty-two additional passengers, not counting numerous serpents, birds, and other exotic creatures, including a number of elephants.

Judith E. Hill provides a vivid description of the steam ship in her book, *Grand Manan, Jewel of the Sea*: "The *Royal Tar* was an odd-looking craft with a hull that was rounded and broad beamed and swept aft with a rising curve that produced a high poop deck with an enormous cabin perched on her stern and windows over her rudder. The vessel had two enormous side wheel propellers, two lofty smokestacks and a touring mast with main and topsails...The vessel's only deck was covered by a vast canvas from the twin smokestacks aft to the stern in the shape of a carnival tent."

The *Royal Tar* had scarcely left the port of St. John when a storm came up which knocked her about and caused considerable damage. She limped into Eastport, Maine, for repairs and an attempt to calm the animals, many of which were half-crazed by their recent ordeal. Repairs having been made, the *Royal Tar* got under way again, only to encounter a second storm off Grand Manan, this one worse than the first. Meanwhile, noticing that the smokestacks of the steam ship were glowing red-hot, the United States Cutter *Veto* kept close by.

Although the pilot on the *Veto* hailed the *Royal Tar* and pointed out the potential for disaster to one of the engineers, the latter dismissed the notion that anything might be amiss. Minutes later smoke began to billow from a partition separating the elephants from the boiler, and the *Royal Tar* was hopelessly ablaze.

As pandemonium broke loose with frantic passengers scurrying for safety amidst exotic snakes and terrified beasts of the jungle, Captain Reed gave orders to abandon ship. In the confusion most of the lifeboats became entangled or capsized. The *Veto*—which was carrying a large amount of gunpowder—kept a prudent distance from the now blazing inferno, but launched a long boat to rescue injured passengers and crew. However, the inexperienced officer in charge of the boat panicked when he came alongside the *Royal Tar* and, turning around, beat a hasty retreat back to the cutter.

The horror of the scene, the screaming passengers and the agonized roaring and screeching of the dying creatures aboard the doomed steam ship, can only be imagined. At one point desperate men tore planks from the burning deck and hastily built and launched a makeshift raft, and paddled with their hands, only to perish when a crazed elephant plunged from the deck onto the raft and sank it.

In an act of unmitigated stupidity, the circus's treasurer tied a money belt—laden with more than five hundred dollars in coins—around his waist, ran to the railing, and leapt overboard. Not surprisingly, he and his money belt immediately sank to the bottom of the Bay of Fundy, where presumably the coins—and his bones—rest to this day.

Nearly half the people aboard the steam ship, and all of the circus creatures, died that day. If there are no ghosts associated with the disaster, there certainly ought to be.◊

Play It Again, Harold

[The Swiss psychologist Carl Gustav Jung, who early in his career did not believe in ghosts,] spent several weekends in a country house in Buckinghamshire which a friend had recently rented. During several nights he heard all sorts of noises—the dripping of water, rustlings, knockings, which increased in intensity until, during the fifth weekend, he thought somebody outside was knocking on the wall with a sledgehammer.

"I had the feeling of a close presence. I opened my eyes with an effort. Then I saw lying next to my head on the pillow, the head of an old woman whose right eye, wide open, was staring at me. The left half of her face was missing. I leapt out of bed and lit a candle." Thereupon the head vanished. Later on, Jung and his host discovered that the whole village knew the house was haunted. It was torn down soon after.
 —*Arthur Koestler,* The Roots of Coincidence

When I first decided to write and publish books of true New England ghost stories I established a hard and fast rule: I would write about only those hauntings that I had myself researched, along with those that I came across—unearthed so to speak—in obscure publications. The one thing I would not do would be to rehash material that was readily available elsewhere.

Well, in this chapter—about a most unusual musical instrument—I break that rule. I do so for several reasons. The hauntings or strange occurrences took place in or around Wareham, Massachusetts, the town on Cape Cod where I was born and where I attended school and worked and lived for more than half my life. And although I know of at least three books which contain its story, most people to whom I mention the haunted violin of Wareham claim never to have heard of it. My final justification, however, for retelling the story is that several years ago I met and talked with one of the principals involved.

For obvious reasons, the days surrounding Halloween are busy ones for writers of true ghost stories and of horror and other weird fiction. On Saturday evening, October 20, in the year 2000, I found myself in Dartmouth, Massachusetts, doing a reading and signing at Baker Books. Sharing the podium, as it were, was another local writer of the mysterious and macabre, Curt Norris, who grew up in Pembroke and was at the time, I believe, living in Norton—and who had already authored a number of books on mysterious happenings in the New England area.

Toward the end of the evening we had a chance to chat and get acquainted. I bought a copy of one of Mr. Norris's books (*Ghosts I Have Known*), and he bought a copy of one of mine (*Shapes That Haunt New England*). As we compared notes, we discovered that we had something in common. We had both, at one time in our lives (though not at the same time in each other's), been employed by the Wareham *Courier*—Mr. Norris as editor, I in the less exalted position of paper boy.

My tenure at the weekly occurred back in the 1950's, when the per copy price was ten cents. Even at that, I remember certain customers on my route who habitually grumbled about the paper's lack of substance—some of whom, along with others less vocal, tried to cheat me, a mere boy, of the ten cents they owed, insisting that they had already paid their dime, when in fact they had not. I don't recall exactly what portion of the money collected each week the paper allowed me to keep, but it wasn't much, hardly worth the hardship and effort of braving the elements, fending off ferocious dogs (there were no leash laws then) and wrangling with hostile customers.

Curt Norris's stint as editor took place sometime in the 1960's, a fact that is pertinent, if only in a peripheral way, to the history of the haunted violin. As I indicated above, the story has been included in at least three books: Norris's own *Ghosts I Have Known*; Robert Ellis Cahill's *New England's Ghostly Haunts*; and *Mysterious New England*, compiled by the editors of *Yankee Magazine*. All three versions repeat roughly the same data. I believe that although his book was the last to appear, Norris was actually the first to write about the violin, if not in the *Courier* itself, then perhaps in the "New England Mysteries" column he used to write for the Quincy *Patriot Ledger*—though not having researched the matter I cannot say for sure. Suffice it to say that his account is the fullest. (For those interested, the only photograph of the violin and its owner appeared in Cahill's book.)

These are the facts, culled from the three accounts:

A well known and respected violinist named Harold Gordon Cudworth collected old violins; he owned between forty and fifty. His prized possession was a violin made in 1769 by Joseph Hornsteiner of Mittenwald, Germany. Judging by its ornate design, consisting of 365 inlaid pieces, the violin had been made for a member of the nobility or perhaps even royalty.

One day in 1945, while playing the instrument in the kitchen of his mother's home in Wareham, Cudworth suddenly heard strange rumbling noises that seemed to emanate from the sink. As soon as he stopped playing, the rumblings ceased. When he began playing again, the rumblings resumed. He jokingly mentioned to his mother, who was present, that the rumblings appeared to be associated with the violin.

The tune he had been playing on the violin was "The Broken Melody," composed by the English cellist Van Biene. Two weeks later, when, while practicing for a concert, he again played "The Broken Melody," he once more heard rumblings, this time from a different part of the house. Thereafter, whenever he played the tune on that same violin he could generally expect (though not always) to experience some sort of poltergeist activity.

Such activity took place one evening in a home in New Bedford. Having given a music lesson to a young pupil, Cudworth was asked by the child's father to remain awhile and play something on his violin. One of the tunes Cudworth selected was "The Broken Melody." As he played—on the third floor of the house—violent rumblings could be heard downstairs.

On another occasion as he played "The Broken Melody" before an audience in a house in Wareham, pictures and other objects hanging on the wall began to sway violently to and fro. Sometimes when Cudworth played the tune in his own home, cups, saucers, and other objects would fly across the room. Over the years numerous people witnessed these and similar phenomena.

Harold Cudworth, Violinist

Perhaps the eeriest event of all happened one night shortly after Cudworth returned home and was preparing to retire for the night. The latch on the attic door began to move up and down—something it had done in the past. But this time the action was so violent that Cudworth went up into the attic to investigate. He found no one there. However, the door to the music cabinet was ajar, and inside, lying on top, was the sheet music for "The Broken Melody."

Cudworth, who was not superstitious and claimed that he did not believe in ghosts, was sixty-one years old and had been enduring the shenanigans of his violin / poltergeist for more than twenty years, when Curt Norris as editor of the Wareham *Courier* invited him to take part in a little experiment. Would he play "The Broken Melody" for a group of newspaper reporters some evening in the *Courier* offices located on Main Street? As Norris states in his book, the offices were "located on the bottom floor of an otherwise empty three-story building."

Cudworth, by all accounts a pleasant, affable man, agreed to the request. However, despite the somewhat spooky atmosphere, when he played before the small gathering of reporters nothing untoward occurred, other than the sound of a door slamming upstairs—in the presumably deserted building. Three of the reporters ventured upstairs and verified that indeed, the top two floors were vacant. Cudworth played the tune again, and then a third time. Finally, the group broke up and everybody went home. Everybody except for the editor. Norris had some work that he wanted to complete before morning.

With this cliffhanger, I'll leave off. Curt Norris told me what happened after the others left. And he skillfully and atmospherically describes the events in his book. It would be unfair of me to steal his thunder, other than to briefly state that he heard noises, including footsteps that crossed the rooms upstairs before beginning to descend the stairs. The intrepid Norris flung open the office door and dashed to the stairwell with his flash camera and took a picture. But there was nothing there.

◇◇◇

Footnote

In the fall of 2003 I gave a talk about local hauntings to a gathering of the Wareham Historical Society. In my talk I included the above essay, in hopes that one or more of the members might be able to shed further light on the subject. Of the thirty-five or so persons present, only a handful had ever heard of Harold Gordon Cudworth and his haunted violin, and none of these had anything substantial to add to the facts already known to me. Someone, however, mentioned that Harold's nephew, William Cudworth, still lived in Wareham and might prove a valuable source of information. Would I want his name and phone number?

Would I, indeed! I had already undertaken some detective work of my own, and had gotten nowhere. My mother—ninety-two years old at the time I talked to her about the haunted violin—remembered Harold Cudworth's *father*. When she was a little girl—this was back around 1920—he used to make ice cream in a shed behind his house and peddle it from a horse-drawn wagon. A cone cost five cents, she recalled. But of the violin she could tell me nothing. Nor could anyone else I questioned.

Bill Cudworth graciously consented to be interviewed in his home. He was able to provide some additional information, though not a great deal, as well as one or two photographs of his uncle playing the violin, but in the end the mystery of Harold Cudworth only deepened.

His uncle married late in life, Bill told me, and spent his later years in Lakeville. He died around 1989—Bill couldn't remember the exact date; "Time passes so quickly," he said. Harold's parents' house, where many of the phenomena associated with the violin occurred, was torn down some years ago to make way for an office complex. It was located off of Route 28, near where the police station is now.

What of the Hornsteiner? I asked. The famous haunted violin. What ever became of it?

Bill didn't know for sure. His uncle gradually sold off most of his collection of rare instruments through an auction house (Skinner's, in Bolton, Massachusetts) and presumably the Hornsteiner was among those auctioned off.

Bill recalled some highlights of his uncle's career as a violinist. He played for a time with an orchestra at Massasoit College in Brockton, and often played at local granges. He made at least one recording, of Christmas carols. This was broadcast over a loud speaker one year in Middleborough center. Bill, though he had heard his uncle perform a number of times, had never witnessed any of the hauntings. And unfortunately he did not own a copy of the record.

Perhaps the most valuable information Bill provided was contained in a magazine article about his uncle which he'd clipped years ago and saved. The article (unfortunately undated), is titled "Has Cape Cod Man Discovered Stradivari's Secret?" It was written by none other than Curtis B. Norris, and was apparently based on an interview he'd conducted with Harold Cudworth. Ah, here was gold indeed!

The article recounts details of Cudworth's early life, his passion for classical music (first heard as a child on those old wax cylinder records that pre-dated flat discs) and his equal passion for the beautifully crafted violins of the old Italian masters. The detail I find most fascinating is this: in 1932 Cudworth had his own half-hour radio program, on WSAR out of Fall River. The show, which featured Cudworth playing the violin, was titled "Out of the Dusk to You." Appropriately named, wouldn't you agree, given his later experiences with "The Broken Melody" and the haunted violin?

However, the main theme of the article is Cudworth's claim that he had discovered the techniques, lost for generations, employed by the old masters—Stradivari, Amati, Guarneri in making the greatest violins the world has ever heard. He claimed that over the years he had "conducted thousands of experiments" in order to discover the secret behind the superior tones produced by the Italian violins of the sixteenth and seventeenth centuries. "I have spent much of my life trying to find the reason for the beautiful mellow, pure, brilliant, and flexible soulful tone of these instruments," he is quoted as saying. "Then, three years ago, I hit upon it—I found the long-sought answer."

However, try as he might, Norris was unable to pry the secret from

Cudworth. No, it wasn't the type of wood used by the old masters, nor the glue, nor the type of varnish they applied, nor their method in applying it. Then what was it? What secret did the old masters employ, that gave their instruments the tonal characteristics that make each surviving violin worth a million dollars or more? "I will never reveal the secrets," Harold Cudworth asserted, and so far as is known, he never did.

Did Harold Cudworth really and truly discover the secrets of the old masters? There can be no doubt that he himself believed that he had. By all accounts he was a quiet, honest, sincere man, not given to idle boasting.

I wonder: is there a possible connection between "The Broken Melody," the haunted violin, and the fact that Harold Cudworth discovered (yet would not reveal) a secret previously lost to the ages? This is pure speculation on my part, of course, but…could a spirit from the past, somehow, directly or indirectly, have spoken to Harold Cudworth, or in some other way revealed the secret?

We'll never know. Whatever the secret was—along with its source—are secrets Harold Cudworth carried with him to the grave.◊

Hard-Hearted Hannah

There was a woods road which took one on and on, always through the woods until you had rounded the island and returned to the starting point…I was alone and had told no one where I was going…
—Hattie Blossom Fritze, Horse and Buggy Days on Old Cape Cod

No, she's not the Vamp of Savannah, made famous by the jazz-age song: so heartless that she would not hesitate to pour water on a drowning man. The Hannah I write of is from the town of Osterville, on Cape Cod. Nor for that matter is she necessarily hard-hearted. She may have been merely an innocent victim, rather than a cruel victimizer. Ultimately, the truth depends on which version of the story you believe.

One version has it that she was an old witch (or more precisely the *ghost* of an old witch) left by Captain Kidd to guard the pirate gold he buried on Grand Island in Osterville sometime in the late seventeenth century.

The old witch guards the pirate gold in this manner: if anyone should be so lucky as to find the location of the treasure, they must not speak while digging, or else Hannah will let out a soul-shattering screech that will frighten them away and haunt them the rest of their days. Thus she has earned the epithet of Hannah Screechum. Of course, there are skeptics who scoffingly claim that the horrific shriek heard by a pair of treasure seekers who rashly uttered "We've found it!" when their spade struck the buried chest was merely the screech of a hoot owl. But so far, these same skeptics have not offered to go and dig up the treasure for themselves.

Another version of the story has it that it was Blackbeard, not Kidd, who buried the treasure—on Oyster, not Grand, Island. An unfortunate young woman named Hannah happened to come upon the buccaneers while they were at work, and although she attempted to escape, she was captured and brutally murdered, and her body flung on top of the chest so that her spirit might guard it through eternity. If anyone approaches the spot where the gold is hidden, Hannah frightens them away with her horrible screeching (an echo, perhaps, of the screams she made while being murdered). This Hannah is known variably as Hannah Screechum or Hannah the Screecher.

Notes

For those a little hazy on their pirates: Blackbeard's real name was Edward Teach. He was a British pirate whose dates are not precisely known, except that he died in 1718. An entry in one of my source books for Captain (William) Kidd informs us that he was a "Scottish-born pirate; hanged" and that his dates are 1645?-1701.◊

At the Keyhole of Eternity

I do not think the universe is a charitable institution, but we have to live in it and make the best of it. The limitations of our biological equipment may condemn us to the role of Peeping Toms at the keyhole of eternity. But at least let us take the stuffing out of the keyhole, which blocks even our limited view.
    —Arthur Koestler, The Roots of Coincidence

The *American Heritage Dictionary of the English Language* defines *coincidence* as "An accidental sequence of events that appear to have a causal relationship." It's an adequate definition, I suppose—good enough for those ordinary, everyday, plain-Jane coincidences we all experience from time to time. You're thinking about dear old Aunt Sarah, whom you haven't heard from in some time, let's say, and suddenly the phone rings and lo and behold! it's Aunt Sarah. Or you're reading a book while listening to the radio and just as your eye falls on the word *spinach* the announcer, talking about salads or Popeye or whatever, speaks—at the exact same moment—the word *spinach*. Both instances are interesting, perhaps, but only in a minor way. Such coincidences are bound to happen and in the end don't mean very much, if they mean anything at all.

But there are some coincidences which in their weirdness, their intricacy (for lack of a better word), transcend the dictionary definition—in fact go way beyond it, seemingly into other realms, other dimensions.

Such a coincidence happened yesterday. While browsing in a used bookstore (Remains To Be Seen in Dartmouth, Massachusetts) I came upon a quaint volume of true ghost stories: *Virginia Ghosts*, by Marguerite DuPont Lee—an inexpensive reprint, from 1966, which comprised two earlier books originally published in the early 1930's. It was an exciting find, full of fascinating tales sure to keep me pleasantly occupied next winter on many a drab evening.

On the title page, in neat handwriting, there was an inscription in bright red ink:

> Dad—
> For reading during the next East-coast blackout (but I hear there isn't a "ghost" of a chance for that to happen again!)
> With love,
> Lynne
> Christmas '69

I glanced at the inscription; read it with amusement, thinking about the time, nearly forty years ago, when in the words of a once popular tune "the lights went out in Massachusetts"; and having paid for the book went outside to the parking lot, where I climbed into my car for the ride home. It was late afternoon on Thursday, August 14, 2003. I turned on the radio for the news. And immediately learned of the massive power outage—the most extensive in American history—that had just occurred, blacking out most of the Northeast and parts of Canada.

"*Not a ghost of a chance*" indeed.

◊◊◊

What exactly—in the meaningful sense—is a coincidence? In what way does the incident described above transcend the ordinary? Let's look at the root of the word. *Coincidence* derives from Medieval Latin: *co-*, together; and *incidere*, to happen. Things—events—happen together.

I purchase a book with an inscription mentioning the major East coast blackout that occurred in 1965, and the unlikelihood that a similar blackout could occur again. Minutes later, I learn that a similar blackout has in fact just occurred. Those are the two things happening together. What makes this coincidence extraordinary is, first, the fact that the inscription occurs in a book of true ghost stories, and contains a pun about "not a ghost of a chance"; and the exact timing of the coincidence. Had I happened upon the book a day earlier, or on the following day, it would still be a coincidence, but not necessarily an exceptional one.

Consider the following, transcribed from a previous book of mine, *Witches of Plymouth County*:

{On November First—the day after Halloween—I gave a talk in Middleborough on the subject of hauntings in southeastern Massachusetts to an audience of approximately sixty-five women. (It would be gratifying to report that the women had gathered for the sole purpose of hearing my presentation, but alas, not so. They were members of a women's club who held regular monthly meetings; I just happened to be that month's guest speaker. My audience was, per force, a captive one.)

I mention this because of what happened after the talk: one of those mind-boggling coincidences that make writing about the paranormal an exciting adventure rather than an onerous chore.

I had spent several hours that morning working on the first part of this chapter—recording what I knew of Witch Rock, and wondering how I could learn more about its history, in particular, who first painted the witch, and why. After the talk, which ended around one o'clock, I lingered with my wife in the hall where the meeting had been held, chatting with members of the audience and signing books. As I was about to leave for home a woman approached. "Are you familiar with Witch Rock, in Rochester?" she asked.

"Yes," I replied, somewhat taken aback. "Funny you should mention it. I'm currently working on a book about witches and I've been doing research on Witch Rock—though without much luck, I'm afraid."

"I grew up in the house on the property where the rock is located. It was my step-mother who painted the witch."

My wife and I exchanged glances. A chill ran up and down my spine. (That cold shiver: it's a cliché but it happens! Quite often, in fact, when your subject is ghosts and the supernatural.)}

In the above, a number of "things" happened together to make it more than just an ordinary coincidence. I had been researching Witch Rock for weeks, but only on that particular morning did I sit down to actually begin writing the chapter. And I was more than a bit frustrated, in that despite my continued efforts I had been able to learn very little about the history of the rock—nothing at all about who first painted the silhouette of the witch.

The talk I gave later that morning was on the subject of ghosts. The woman who volunteered the invaluable information I was seeking had not known in advance what the topic would be. In fact, she confessed that when she heard that I would be talking about ghosts she had been tempted to get up and leave the room.

What are the chances that someone in the audience would know the information I sought, let alone be someone who grew up and lived on the property and was the step-daughter of the person who painted the witch? What are the chances that, not knowing that I was writing about Witch Rock (I hadn't referred to it in my talk), she would come up to me afterward and broach the subject?

I don't know about you, but it gives *me* the willies.

A coincidence that did not give me the willies, but which is worthy of note, is the first of any significance that I can recall. Briefly:

In the 1970's I bought a house in the section of West Wareham, Massachusetts, known as Finn Town. Since I was one of the first persons of non-Finnish heritage to live there (several of my new neighbors spoke Finnish as their first language), my friends and relatives had been kidding me about my new residence, with puns and gibes and what have you. On the evening of the day I moved in, tired from my exertions, I sat in the living room listening to a classical music station on the radio and reading *The New Yorker*. As I idly turned the pages of the magazine my eyes fell on the word Finlandia, in an ad for vodka of that name. Simultaneously, the music came to a close and the announcer named it: *Finlandia*, by the Finnish composer Jean Sibelius. The announcer spoke the word *Finlandia* at the precise moment my eyes fell on the word in the ad.

This, certainly, was more than just an ordinary coincidence. First, I was conscious of being in Finn Town. Second, the folks at the radio station chose that evening to play *Finlandia*, certainly a popular classical work, but not one heard all that often. Third, I chose, that evening, to read *The New Yorker*, which contained an ad for a vodka named Finlandia. No big deal, perhaps—except the uncanny timing. Had I come across the ad shortly before or after the piece had been played on the radio, I would have thought it a coincidence, pleasant enough, but not one worthy of note. It was the precise simultaneity of the events that evoked a feeling of awe, and still does to this day.

◊◊◊

Several years ago while I was working on *Haunters of the Dusk*, a collection of true New England ghost stories, not one, but two weird coincidences occurred. Both were in keeping with the subject matter.

One of the book's chapters, titled "The House of the Five Suicides," is about an ancient house in Middleborough, Massachusetts—which together with its surrounding acreage seems to attract more than its share of suicides. I won't repeat the details here, except to say that troubled people seem drawn to the property. One evening while I was putting the polishing touches to the chapter on "The House of the Five Suicides" I received an excited phone call from the woman who owns and lives in the house.

"All afternoon helicopters have been hovering over the place," she said. "Finally, this evening my daughter went outside to see what the commotion was all about, and one of the 'copters shone a spotlight on her. She came inside and phoned a friend who works for one of the local police departments. Her friend told her they're looking for a man who's missing and believed to be suicidal."

A week later hunters found the man's body hanging from a tree.

The dedication to *Haunters of the Dusk* reads: "To Dorothy for her friendship and patience and for sharing her stories, and to Norman and Doug." Dorothy is Dorothy Massey; Norman is her husband, and Doug is their son. Norman is related to the actor, Raymond Massey (famous among other things for his portrayal of Abraham Lincoln). Dorothy has had many encounters with ghosts (she prefers the term *spirits*). Although she does not claim to posses psychic powers, it sometimes seems as though she has, on some subconscious level, the ability to read minds, or perhaps it would be more accurate to say, to link her mind with the thoughts of others.

Case in point: One evening several years ago, while *Haunters of the Dusk* was still a work in progress, I happened to be leafing through a book I had recently acquired called *I Believe in Ghosts*; it consists of true ghost stories told to the author, Danton Walker, by famous people—actors and other celebrities. (It's a re-edited version of an earlier book called *Spooks Deluxe*, originally published in 1956.)

The phone rang. My wife answered it. I heard her say, "Oh, hello, Dorothy." At precisely that moment my eyes fell on the name *Dorothy Massey*, whose story about a haunting experienced by her and her famous husband, Raymond, Walker had included in his book.

It was of course our friend Dorthy Massey on the phone. We had not seen or spoken with her in the past few weeks, yet she chose that moment to phone us—the exact moment that my eyes fell on the name of her long deceased relative-by-marriage, a name that varies from hers by only one letter. And of course the subject matter in the book was ghosts.◊

King Philip's Head

The beautiful eminence of Mount Hope was the ancient seat of Philip, the great sachem of the Wampanoags. When his reverses had left him only a handful of followers, Philip took the sublime resolution of returning to his mountain home and dying like a chief of royal blood, with his arms in his hands. Mount Hope was quickly surrounded by his enemies; and the dreaded warrior fell, shot through the heart by a renegade of his own race.
    —Samuel Adams Drake, New England Legends and Folklore

Suddenly one of the waiting pairs spotted an Indian racing toward them in silence, running for his very life from the pursuing white men. They stood together in readiness, this pair—one an Englishman, the other an Indian. At the right moment, when their target was within range, the white man pulled his trigger, but the gun failed to function. Thereupon his Indian companion opened fire, and the fleeing enemy spun forward upon his face. Elated, the two men advanced to have a closer look at the twisted and motionless form sprawled there in the mud. When they peered at the begrimed and contorted features, they recognized King Philip—dead.
    —Douglas Edward Leach,
    Flintlock and Tomahawk: New England in King Philip's War

King Philip's War (1675-1676) has been referred to, among other things, as America's forgotten war; the bloodiest war ever fought on American soil; and America's first great war of extermination. And indeed it is all of these. Even though it is one of this country's most important wars, in that it changed the course of history in the New World (setting back European colonization in New England by at least fifty years, while at the same time ending forever any serious challenge to further expansion presented by the native population), its history is familiar to some only vaguely, and to many others not at all. It has earned the designation as America's bloodiest war, not because of actual numbers killed (the Civil War holds that record) but because of the percentage of the total population (both English and Indian) who perished as a result of the conflict. And it is the first great war of extermination (there had been lesser wars previously) because much of the Indian population in New England died either during combat or massacres (perpetrated against women and children as well as able-bodied warriors), as a result of interment in camps (into which peaceful—so-called praying Indians—were forced and where, shamelessly ill-treated, hundreds died), or by execution after the war (the Indians were treated as traitors rather than as enemy combatants and were daily hanged, ten or twenty at a time, long after the war ended) or were sold into slavery (as far away as the West Indies, and even Morocco).

As one might expect, such a tragic, bloody affair has over the centuries given rise to countless legends and tales of hauntings and other supernatural occurrences. I included one such tale, "A Relique from King Philip's War," about a present-day haunting in Middleborough connected to an actual event that took place at the outbreak of the war, in a previous book, *Haunters of the Dusk*. And I've used material from King Philip's War as background for a number of fictional ghost stories.

So I was especially pleased the other day, while signing books at a craft show in Raynham, Massachusetts, to hear still another ghost story pertinent to "America's forgotten war," this one involving none other than King Philip himself. A woman who approached our table to purchase a book (not one of mine—one of my wife's cookbooks, but I'll forgive her for that!) got to chatting with us, and mentioned that she was glad to read our motto, "Preserving Our New England Heritage," which we have emblazoned on a banner attached to our table.

"Too many of our stories and legends are being lost to future generations," she said. "It's good to see someone like yourself writing some of them down for our children and grandchildren to enjoy. These stories are an important part of their New England heritage."

The subject then turned to King Philip's War. "You know," she said, "King Philip's ghost haunts this area. He appears skulking about in the woods and swamps in and around Raynham every three to five years—looking for his head. The Indians believed that in order to move on to the next world the body had to be whole. When he was killed, Philip was quartered, and his head was sent to Plymouth where it was impaled on a stake to serve as a warning to others."

"Yes," I said. "Supposedly it—or his skull—was still there twenty years after the war."

"Well," she said, "maybe not. There's a tradition that some members of my family living here in Raynham were friends of Philip's. They somehow got hold of his head and preserved it in a jar and hid it in their cellar. And," she added, "recently during renovations in the courthouse in Taunton a head pickled in a jar was discovered. It was sent away to be examined, and was determined to be the head of a native American."

That, essentially, is the story the woman told me, though since I wasn't taking notes I may have got some of the details wrong. I neglected to ask whether those ancestors of hers who were friends of Philip were English or Indian, but I suspect the former. Before the war Philip had many friends among the settlers, and it is highly unlikely that any Indians who survived the war would have been in a position to obtain his head. In any event, it's an interesting story. As the woman walked away she mentioned that Philip's ghost was about due to make one of its periodic visitations. "Maybe I'll get to see him this time," she said.◊

The Tortured Tree

The Peace of Old New England Cemeteries

*The peace you'll find when finally dead
is quite unlike the peace you find,
while still alive,
in old New England cemeteries*

*where the Dead, long decayed,
lie absolutely still
amid surrounding woods*

*and the stones
that weigh upon their graves
have sunk to rakish angles
or lie embedded in the roots of trees,*

*names and dates once deeply etched
obscured now by soft lichen*

and the weatherings of time.

The old burying ground on Ben Abbey Road off of historic Route 6A in Bourne, on Cape Cod, is worth a visit for those who respect and enjoy "the peace of old New England cemeteries." It's a quiet place to spend an hour or two, perhaps in the morning or early evening, and contemplate the meaning of life and of death; or refreshen your sense of history by reading the grave markers and marveling at the varied lives led by those who came before us; or just sit and watch the many birds as they flit from tree to tree.

There is one old tree in the cemetery, gnarled and twisted, that is reputed to be haunted, that is to say, inhabited by a ghost. I don't know the full details of the story, except that color photos of the tree are said to sometimes show a blue aura around it. Another writer, I'm told, has been researching the story, so I will not trespass upon his territory, other than to say that the tree's peculiar deformities suggest that it may indeed harbor a restless spirit.

Though no expert, I believe the tree is some type of poplar: a quaking aspen, perhaps, though that would be too much to expect, too neat a fit for this story. More likely it is an eastern cottonwood. An interesting experiment for the curious would be to visit the cemetery at twilight, some winter's eve, and respectfully wait for the ghost to appear.◊

The Tortured Tree

The Bogman's Tale

...a death in the family was told to the bees, and sometimes the hives were trimmed with crepe, as if it were possible for the wandering spirit of the dead to come back to the homestead to get a supply of honey, if stinted of it in the last resting-place.
—William Root Bliss, The Old Colony Town
and the Ambit of Buzzards Bay

◇◇◇

"Even though it was late summer and the blossoms had already set, the bee hives which the company had rented for the season hadn't been removed; there were thirty of 'em, lined up in trim rows...on the clearing...

"As luck would have it one of the hives decided to swarm. Evidently the colony had prospered and outgrown itself. The first queen to hatch had stung the others to death, had mated with a drone, and was ready to set up housekeeping elsewhere.

"I was the first to spot 'em, a black smear against the sky, ragged at the edges like a miniature twister.

"'Look out, boys,' I shouted. 'If the queen chooses you as a likely roost the others will, too. All ten thousand of 'em.'"
—Edward Lodi, Deep Meadow Bog

Our ancestors believed in the sagacity of bees. The high regard in which they held these fascinating insects came about, no doubt, from centuries of observation: bees are industrious; they wander far afield in search of nectar but always find their way back to the hive; they manufacture a valuable substance, honey, and provide ahead for the lean winter months; they have a complex social system headed by a queen. The practice of "telling the bees"—of notifying the hives of any important event taking place in a household, such as a betrothal, marriage, birth, or death—is believed to be thousands of years old, dating far back into prehistory.

Informing the bees of a death in the family was held to be of particular importance. Failure to do so might cause the bees to swarm and leave the premises, with the resultant loss by the family of their precious honey (throughout the ages, before the introduction of processed sugar, mankind's only sweetener). This superstition at one time may have been relevant only to the person who actually tended to the hives; surely, if that person died and the bees were not told, they would not understand why they were not being cared for, and as a consequence would leave. Some folks carried the superstition further; they believed that when the beekeeper died, if the bees swarmed they were following his soul.

Throughout the centuries many other superstitions concerning bees have evolved. Under no circumstances must a menstruating woman touch a beehive; were she to do so, all the bees would immediately fly away, never to return. However, whenever a new swarm is placed into a hive, insert the blade of a knife under the lid, and the bees will never fly away. Should a swarm of bees settle on your property, be sure to claim them as your own; otherwise a death in the family or some other calamity is sure to occur within the year. If a bee flies through an open window into your house, rejoice; it is a sign that good fortune will soon follow. Kill a bee on the first day of May, keep it with you in your pocket or purse, and you will never be without funds.

What, the reader may be wondering, does all of this bee lore—

interesting though it may be—have to do with the subject of ghosts? The answer: very little, or a great deal—depending on how you interpret the story that was told to me one summer afternoon at a craft fair where my wife and I were exhibiting our books, and which I will repeat here. The story was told to me by a man who, reluctant to be perceived by his friends and acquaintances as someone who believes in ghosts, asked to be identified only as "a Finn from Carver."

Though "Finn" is no doubt an ethnic designation, I'll henceforth refer to my interlocutor as Mr. Finn.

"I'm a bogman. A cranberry grower," Mr. Finn informed me. "As you know, bog owners keep bees around their bogs to pollinate the crops. The honey produced by the hives is only a byproduct. The real value of the bees is in helping the cranberry blossoms to set.

"Most of the growers rent hives from professional beekeepers. The beekeepers set up the hives, tend to them, move them if necessary—for which they get paid (and also get to keep all the honey). My situation, though, was a little different. My foreman—we'll call him Harry—was also a beekeeper. That is to say he dabbled in bees, more as a hobby than as a way to make money, though I paid him the going rate, and he also made a small profit from selling the honey.

"It's not everyone, of course, who's willing to work around bees. No matter how careful you try to be you're bound to get stung occasionally. Me, I'm allergic to bees and could swell up and die if I got stung. I was more than happy to have Harry on hand to care for the hives. With a regular beekeeper, the grower has to wait for service. But with Harry, if I wanted the hives moved from one location to another, I'd just have to mention it, and Harry would do it for me right away.

"You ever see a beekeeper at work?" Mr. Finn asked.

I told him I had, many a time, when I worked on the bogs. "They look like some sort of monster, or an alien from outer space, like you used to see in those old science fiction or horror flics from the fifties," I said, "got up in their baggy outfits, with protective helmets of wire mesh netting over their heads, and squirting smoke into the hives." (The hives, constructed from wood and painted white to reflect the heat in summer, from the outside resemble plain boxes; the smoke—produced from smoldering wood chips or damp hay and squirted from a device that resembles a coffee can with a long spout—is used to calm the bees into submission.)

"Half the time Harry didn't bother with the outfit," Mr. Finn said. "Said it was too much hassle. Claimed if you handled the bees properly you didn't need protective clothing." He shrugged. "For him, it worked. He didn't mind getting stung. He claimed he had built up an immunity."

At this point Mr. Finn got on with his story: "One day, it was late August, a few weeks before harvest, I was driving my pickup along a dike near the clearing where that spring Harry had placed a number of hives, stopping now and then to check on the crop, and with an eye out for muskrat damage. The bees had already done their work for the season, of course. Any day now Harry would move the hives to another location, away from the vines, so as not to pose a hazard for the workers during harvest.

"I parked the pickup on the dike a safe distance from the hives and jumped the ditch to see how the crop was ripening. I stooped over and ran my fingers through the vines, turning the berries over to check their color. When I straightened, I saw something out of the corner of my eye, a shadow maybe, moving along the shore, and then I recognized it for what it was: one of the hives had swarmed. The colony had grown too large and part of it, headed by a new queen, was leaving to establish a second colony elsewhere.

"'I'd better go find Harry,' I thought. 'He'll want to catch this swarm before it gets away.' He'd do that by following it until it landed somewhere and then nabbing the queen. Once you've got the queen the rest of the swarm follows. But hell, you know all about that," Mr. Finn said.

"But even as I looked," he went on, "I saw that there was something peculiar about this particular swarm. Now, here's where it all becomes uncertain—in my mind, that is. You can argue that what I saw I only *think* I saw—because of how things turned out. What I think I saw—no, what I *know* I saw—is this: the swarm had formed itself into a recognizable shape.

I swear to God it had taken on the shape of a hangman's noose. I didn't get that impression afterwards; I got it then and there."

He shook his head. "Maybe you can understand why I don't want my name mentioned in connection with this. People might think I'm nuts, or just making it up to call attention to myself, and in light of what happened, I wouldn't want them to think that."

He paused as if to weigh his words carefully, then plunged ahead with the story.

"You know that test psychiatrists use, where you look at an abstract drawing and interpret what you see?"

"The Rorschach test," I said.

"Right. Well, if you've ever seen bees swarm maybe you'll get my drift. Thousands of bees moving all at once, rapidly, in a writhing mass, like an abstract painting, only three-dimensional. See what I mean? It's like lying in the grass and staring at the clouds as they drift overhead. Gaze at the sky long enough and you begin to see different shapes. A giraffe, maybe, or a pirate ship, or an old man with a beard.

"So at first I thought, 'My mind is playing tricks. I just think I see a hangman's noose. Pretty soon I'll be seeing something else. Who knows, maybe a baby carriage or a French poodle.' I got into my pickup, all the while keeping an eye on the swarm, to let Harry know what direction they were heading in. I drove to the end of the dike, turned around, and headed back toward the clearing where the hives were. Harry was in the area somewhere, mowing with the tractor. Even if I lost sight of the swarm Harry would probably be able to find the bees before they settled in to their new location.

"But I tell you, I was getting the creeps. That swarm just seemed to hover there, if anything looking more than ever like a hangman's noose. As I approached, it began (still holding its shape) to move—in the direction I was headed in, toward a bay of the bog that was hidden from view by a stand of trees. That's where I thought Harry might be, and sure enough, as I rounded the bend I saw his tractor parked outside an old storage shed. Harry, though, was nowhere in sight.

"That was strange. The shed was dilapidated, at least a hundred years old, and dated back to the horse-and-buggy days when harvested berries often had to be stored for days at a time before being carted to the screen house. These days we used it mostly for storing rakes and shovels and other odd tools. Why would Harry be parked next to it?

"And why did the swarm of bees lead me to it, and then just hover nearby, in that hangman's knot?

"Can you guess what I found inside that shed when I opened the door?" Mr. Finn asked.

"I think I can," I answered. "But you tell me."

"I found Harry hanging from a rafter. He'd hanged himself. He'd always had a drinking problem, and I guess his wife had left him, and he just decided to end it all. In a panic I cut him down. But it was too late. He was dead. It's not a pretty sight, a man who's hanged himself, and I suppose you could argue that it was the shock of finding him like that that gave me the idea of the bees beforehand taking on the shape of a noose. But I know what I saw, and I know that I saw it before I ever had a notion that Harry had done himself in."

The Ghost of Brunswick High

Those who die violently are the most likely to be foot-loose after death—those drowned at sea, killed in railroad, automobile, and industrial accidents, killed in battle, and most especially those who are murdered or commit suicide.
   —Louis C. Jones, THINGS THAT GO BUMP IN THE NIGHT

The title of this brief chapter is a pun of sorts, or at least a play on words. For sure, there is a ghost that stalks the halls of the building that once housed the high school in Brunswick, Maine. She has been "experienced" by any number of people, including some level-headed and decidedly unsuperstitious teachers. Her name is Mimi, purportedly a student who many years ago fell to her death from the balcony in the auditorium. Whenever her spirit became active, it was rumored, tragedy was bound to strike a student or someone else associated with the school. You can read all about Mimi and her kindred spirits in a book called *Maine Ghosts & Legends*, by Thomas A. Verde.

The book was first published in 1989. Since then the high school has moved to another location; the building now stands empty and

Brunswick High School

deserted, though a section is occasionally used for meetings by one or more civic organizations. To my knowledge, though, no one is ever brave enough to remain there alone at night, for fear of encountering Mimi and provoking the curse, or whatever it may be, that portends death or other misfortune.

With time, the building itself has become a ghost. Walking its grounds even by day, as I did one morning in late September, 2004, can give one the creeps. It's not just Mimi—the notion that she might be peering at you from an upper window, one of those not boarded up— that creates a feeling of unease. There's something else, something vague and undefinable, almost a feeling of impending doom.

Oh well, perhaps that something is only the thought of time passing—symbolized by the old, vacant seat of learning with its crumbling facade—and the doom that awaits us all.◊

The Man in the Three-Cornered Hat

He wore a three-cornered hat, a boat-cloak wrapped round him and sea-boots. But for the fact that he had two legs he might have been Long John Silver himself.
—R.H. Malden, "The Coxswain of the Lifeboat"

◇◇◇

From the summit of the island the view was superb, embracing on one side the ocean dotted with sails, and on the other, across the little roadstead where our vessel lay amid its kindred craft, the pleasant groves and fertile fields of Bailey's Island, and beyond, the far-stretching peninsulas of Harpswell and the countless isles of the bay.
—Robert Carter, A Summer Cruise on the Coast of New England, *1858*

It was legends of the famed Dead Ship, and the hope of learning more about the ghostly vessel—and perhaps even catching a glimpse of it—that first lured me to Harpswell, Maine. What kept me there (for an all too brief stay) was the natural beauty of the peninsulas and islands, the picturesque harbors with their working waterfronts, the historic landmarks, the fabulous food, and the many ghost stories the good people of Harpswell were willing to share.

The risk of converting this book of true New England ghost stories into a travelogue prevents me from expounding any further on the area's many fine features, except to say that one could scarcely do better than to eat at Cook's Lobster House, on Bailey Island, and enjoy the view of the world's only remaining cribstone bridge. (Yes, the off chance of catching a glimpse of the Dead Ship—which hasn't been seen since 1866—seems like a flimsy excuse for pigging out on lobster and drinking fine ales, but there you have it.)

◇◇◇

A town's library is always a good starting point when seeking out local ghosts. Harpswell actually boasts two libraries, though the limited hours of each made it possible for Yolanda and me to visit only one.

Cundy's Harbor Library is the most diminutive library I've ever stepped into. It reminds me of the old one-room school houses that have just about disappeared from the American scene, though it's small

Cundy's Harbor Library

even by that standard. The library at Cundy's Harbor consists of one room, or maybe two, if you count the tiny office space to the left as you enter. There's a fireplace but no indoor facilities. I can't say whether there was ever an outhouse associated with the building, but at present there is, in a rather conspicuous place off to one side, a portable john.

Cundy's Harbor Library is a cozy, inviting place. It was made even more so by the volunteer librarian, Ann Greene, who greeted us warmly and went out of her way to provide us with information about the area as well as leads for further explorations.

"The bed and breakfast up the road has a ghost," she informed us.

Oddly enough, before our trip Yolanda and I had considered staying at that very bed and breakfast, but had been unable to book rooms for the two nights we were to be in Harpswell. After chatting with Ann for the better part of an hour, and leafing through books of interest, we headed directly to The Captain's Watch, which was only a short distance away.

The following, taken from the B & B's website, aptly describes the historic house and its surroundings: "Perched atop the most elevated bluff on the point, 250 feet from the water, this gracious 1862 landmark home affords long views over an authentic small working harbor and beyond to ledges, islands, river and bays. From the octagonal cupola crowning our rooftop, the panoramic vista to the Atlantic is stunning. Sparkling water showered with buoys provides a colorful confetti background for watching lobster boats, sailing vessels, seals and shorebirds."

Ignoring the "No vacancy" sign, Yolanda boldly knocked at the door. It was promptly answered by a distinguished looking gentlemen who graciously admitted us into the house. We identified ourselves and stated our purpose. Even though he was battling the effects of a bad cold, our host led us—two complete strangers—into the parlor, where he took the time to regale us with stories of ghosts and hauntings.

Ken Brigham is a graduate of Bowdoin College and a retired Psychological Examiner. He and his partner, Donna Dillman (a former Dental Hygiene professor, who regrettably was not at home the day of our visit) have been innkeepers since 1986. Throughout our interview Ken emphasized that, in the hauntings he has witnessed or otherwise been privy to, he has never experienced anything evil. "Overwhelming, perhaps. But not evil."

His first experience with the supernatural occurred back in the '70's, when he was living in Cape Elizabeth. While lying in bed one night he saw the spectral form of a young woman in a nightgown. He later learned that back in the 1920's a young woman had committed suicide at that site by jumping off a cliff.

Later he and Donna bought a house in Phippsburg, dating back to the 1770's, which they converted into a bed and breakfast. One night in the master bedroom Ken saw the figure of a man wearing a three-cornered hat. Guests would often report that they felt a presence in that same room. After eleven years, Ken and Donna moved to Harpswell and rented the house in Phippsburg as a B&B. One morning they received a phone call from the new host. He told them that guests staying in the master bedroom said: "You have a female ghost sitting in a rocking chair. *And a man wearing a three-cornered hat.*" (Interestingly enough, there was no actual rocking chair in the room.) Back in the 1770's the house had been a tavern. One modern-day guest remarked: "There are so many presences here. So many people drinking and carrying on."

The Captain's Watch was built during the Civil War as the Union Hotel. It didn't do well—too many men were off fighting the war—but it later flourished, first as the Cliff House, and then as the Ocean View House.

One woman guest who stayed in the suite upstairs, over the living room, awoke during the night and, opening her eyes, saw the figure of a man hovering over her. Presumably his intentions were not honorable. She said to him: "I don't like this. Go away." Obligingly, he vanished.

Other guests in the suite have reported seeing a male figure watching them. One morning a man lying in bed said to his wife: "Do you see…" and she finished the sentence with: "…the man standing by the door?"

Ken and Donna freely allow guests to go into rooms that are currently not booked. Late one night a man, apparently restless, left his own room and wandered into the suite, which was vacant at the time. Though the room was dark he dimly made out the outline of a female figure. "What are you doing here?" she asked.

Sometimes the ghost of a dog is seen at the foot of the bed.

No spectral activity, however, has been reported in the past year and a half.

The Captain's Watch

As for the Dead Ship, we never did catch sight of it—all the more reason to return as soon as possible to Harpswell, stay a day or two at the Captain's Watch, and feast on lobster and down a few ales at Cook's Lobster House.◊

Tales and Ales

What I am about to relate is so marvelous, so weird and startling, that even now, as I dwell upon it all, I wonder why I of all men should have been subjected to the unnatural and unearthly influence. I no longer scoff when somebody reminds me that there is more in heaven and earth than is dreamt of in our philosophy.
—*Dick Donovan, "The Corpse Light"*

The British developed India Pale Ale in the late 1700's for shipment to their troops stationed in India. The voyage from Great Britain to Asia took a number of months, much of that time spent on the high seas under broiling tropical suns. It took a potent ale, with a relatively high alcohol content, to survive such a voyage. The fact that the ale was shipped in sturdy oak casks added to the brew's robust flavor.

Hearty ales and ghosts go well together, a fact demonstrated not too long ago when my wife and I needed some work done on our alarm system. It was Gordon who showed up in the late afternoon, made the necessary changes, and stayed on for a half hour or so afterwards when we discovered that we had a mutual interest: true New England ghost stories. We offered him an ale, which he accepted, and then listened to the stories he had to offer, of some of the hauntings he's encountered over the years.

One twelve-ounce bottle of ale, no matter how robust, is not sufficient to loosen one's tongue in the conventional sense. But there is something about sharing an old-fashioned brew that is conducive to loquacity. And the ale I offered Gordon that day was an Ipswich I.P.A., which features on the bottle the (somewhat ghostly) outline in white of an old sailing vessel. Perhaps it was the image of that tall ship that called to Gordon's mind the first story he related to Yolanda and me.

Hawthorne Street in the old port city of New Bedford has many stately mansions that date from the nineteenth century. In one of them, an old captain's house, Gordon made an interesting discovery.

He was alone in the house installing an alarm system. "You can often tell if a building is haunted," he said, "and there was a definite feeling about that particular dwelling." The first strange thing that occurred was really a series of events. Gordon was using an electric drill. Every so often the drill would stop working, and Gordon would discover that the cord had been unplugged from the wall socket.

"There was no tension on the cord. There was plenty of slack, with loops coiled on the floor. And the plug wasn't loose; it fitted firmly into the outlet. Someone—or some *thing*—was yanking out the plug."

Gordon kept a radio playing while he worked. Every so often the station would change of its own volition. "The radio had a knob that had to be turned in order to tune into another station. As I was working I'd suddenly hear a *blrrrp*, as if someone had rapidly turned the knob past a number of stations, and the radio would be suddenly turned to an entirely different station.

"I had to do some wiring in a crawl space under the eaves. It was a difficult place to access. While I was up there I came upon an old metal box, tucked into a tight corner. Obviously someone had gone to a great deal of trouble to hide it. 'What treasure have I found?' I wondered.

"I shook the box. There was definitely something inside."

The precious items that someone had so carefully hidden a century ago turned out, disappointingly, to be nothing more than compound pills.

"What are compound pills?" I asked Gordon. "I'm not familiar with the term."

"There was a description on the box," Gordon replied. "Evidently they were used to induce an abortion."

In the nineteenth century abortions were illegal and considered highly immoral—tantamount to murder. "Perhaps," I suggested to Gordon, "it was a burden of guilt that prompted an uneasy spirit to make its presence known to you that day."

◊◊◊

Another story of interest that Gordon told us that afternoon pertains to a house in Lakeville, Massachusetts.

"The house is located on Long Pond. I know the present owner. There's not much to the story, really. It seems that one of the previous owners, for whatever reason, crawled under the house to die. The place he crawled to was actually a space located behind another crawl space, not an easy place to get to. I can't say what induced him to go there, but that's were his body was found. The strange thing is, sometime later a workman had to crawl to the same location for some job he was doing on the house. He crawled in, but he never crawled out. He was found there, dead.

"That's about all there is to the story. Except that the present owner was bedridden with a back ailment one winter. From his bedroom he could look out into the room where the Christmas tree was set up. Every so often he would see a form, or figure, pass in front of the tree." Gordon shrugged. "He couldn't say whether there was any connection between the ghost he kept seeing and the two men who died in the crawl space. But it does make you wonder."

◊◊◊

Gordon saved his best story for last.

"Years ago a friend of mine bought an old house on Snipatuit Road in Rochester. The place has a lot of history behind it. Originally it was a stage coach house; after that it became a boy's school for a number of years. I considered buying the place myself, but it needed too much work.

"My friend fixed it up and invited me over for a tour. The house has a lot of features which he's proud of: an old sandstone sink, a Glenwood stove, to mention a couple. You can see that the house was once a school by the railings that go up to the second floor. They're only this high"—Gordon demonstrated by holding his hand a short distance above the floor—"just the right height for small boys."

"The day he showed me the house we looked at the basement, then went up to the first floor. As we passed an old rocking chair I did a double take—you know, looked at the rocker, glanced away, then quickly looked again, not believing what my eyes saw.

"My friend noticed my reaction and asked, 'What was that all about?'

"I said, 'You're not going to believe this, but I saw someone sitting in that chair. A man with a white beard, and with some sort of black hat that went around his head. You know, like the Quakers used to wear.'

"My friend was quiet for a moment, then said: 'I believe you. This morning when I was outside chatting with my neighbor he asked me what I was doing up in the attic so late last night. I told him I hadn't gone near the attic. Oh yes you did, he said. I distinctly saw someone looking out your attic window. It had to be you. You were wearing some sort of black hat.'"◊

The Haunted Library

The Nipmuck Indians had always been friendly with the colony until stirred up by Toby, a Woodstock Indian, who was supported by the Canadian authorities. On the afternoon of Aug. 25th, 1696, the Nipmucks, led by Toby, stealthily approached the house of John Johnson, an Englishman who had married the daughter of Andre Sigourné. The house stood somewhat distant from the others, and its site is marked at the present time with a stone tablet. The savages seized the three young children, Andrew, Peter and Mary, and dashed their heads against the stones of the fireplace. Mrs. Johnson fled from her house in great terror and grief, and aided by her cousin Daniel Johonnot, started toward Woodstock, whither her husband had gone on business. The Woodstock trail divided into two paths, and Mrs. Johnson took the path other from that over which her husband was returning. He was killed by the savages. The Huguenots were so terrified by this sad happening that, after burying the victims, they bundled up as many as possible of their household goods and returned to Boston.

—Celebration of the Town of Oxford, Massachusetts

As the foregoing tragic episode from its early history indicates, Oxford, Massachusetts —like so many New England towns—has a rich and storied past. You can research that past in the Oxford Public Library, where the staff are all friendly and helpful, the surroundings are comfortable, and the resident ghost only occasionally makes a nuisance of herself.

Oxford Public Library

Yolanda and I first heard about the haunted library while exhibiting books at the 2004 Massachusetts Library Conference held on Cape Cod, in Falmouth. Eager to learn more, at the first opportunity, just a few weeks later, we headed for the central part of the state to get the full story.

Director Timothy Kelley—though he himself seemed reluctant to discuss the possibility that his library boasts one or more ghosts—graciously allowed Yolanda and me to interview his staff, having arranged beforehand for us to meet with Scott, the custodian who—brave soul!—spends part of his shift alone in the library after closing hours at night.

When we arrived Brenna Pomeroy set aside her duties at the front desk and gave us a brief tour of the building. We began in the older section, admiring the stained glass windows, the ornate woodwork, and the fireplace that graces the periodical room. A description of the original library (extracted from a book privately published by the Historical Commission in 1988) follows: "The cornerstone for the building was laid in 1903 with the Masonic Grand Lodge of Massachusetts in charge of the ceremonies...The library building is in the form of a Roman Cross and Renaissance in architectural style. Faced with yellow brick, a distinct feature is its stained glass window commemorating 'The Departure of the Pilgrims from Holland in 1620.' The window was designed by Redding, Baird and Company of Boston and is about eight to ten feet in size and located above the main entrance...A museum is located in the basement containing many historic items donated through the years."

"The new section of the library was completed in 2000," Brenna informed us. "All of the hauntings seem to occur in the older part." Indeed, everyone we interviewed that day repeated the same refrain: it is only the original part of the building that is haunted.

I asked Brenna how long she'd worked there.

"About two years," she replied.

And had she experienced anything unusual?

"Just once. It was in the evening around eight-thirty. The library was closed. I was alone downstairs. The only other person in the building was my co-worker, Cheryl, upstairs. I heard a female voice ask, 'Is that her?' and another voice reply, 'No, it's not.' I called up to Cheryl and

The haunted stairway

told her what had happened. She called down, 'Don't tell me that!' because she'd been having experiences of her own."

Cheryl Hansen, we knew, was now director of the library in the neighboring town of Sutton. Although we were not able to interview her in person, Yolanda spoke to her by phone the following day. Cheryl had a number of interesting stories to tell.

We had already heard about the former children's story-time room upstairs: how, since the new addition, it has been used only as attic space for storage. Even though the door to the room is always closed and secured at night, in the morning it is frequently found open. This happened even before Scott began working at the library, and has happened a number of times since. More than one staff member ventured the opinion that perhaps the ghost resents the fact that the space is no longer used as a children's room.

Cheryl reinforced that conjecture when she told Yolanda of a recurring phenomenon, something that happened several times between 1994 and 2000, before the new addition, when the attic room was still the children's room. She would leave at closing time with the books all in order. In the morning, however, (when she was the first one in) she sometimes found that one of the books had been taken from its place on the shelf and positioned on top of the others. It was always the same book: *Cornstalks and Cannonballs*, a fictional work set during the War of 1812.

One rainy Memorial Day Cheryl watched the parade, then decided to take some videos from the library. The building was locked, of course, but she had a key, and shutting off the security system she went inside. As she was busy downstairs going through the videos she could hear someone upstairs, walking around. On another occasion she was upstairs, alone, and heard footsteps. She turned, and out of her peripheral vision she saw a figure in a long black dress.

And once, after hours, not long after the new addition was completed, Cheryl was upstairs by herself, studying for her master's degree. There was no one else in the library. And yet she could hear men's voices, downstairs, in the area of the circulation desk. She hurried down to investigate. There was nobody there.

She left to run some errands. When she returned, Scott had arrived. When she told him of the incident, he said: "Haven't I been telling you for years that I keep hearing voices!"

Shortly before leaving Oxford to assume the directorship of the Sutton Free Public Library, Cheryl witnessed one of the library's more interesting "incidents." As Joshua, a child about three years of age, was on the stairway with his mother, he said: "There's the lady from downstairs."

"What lady?" his mother asked.

"The lady in the picture on the wall."

According to staff members, Joshua has on more than one occasion pointed to the stairway and said, "There's where the ghost lady lives."

The picture that little Joshua referred to is a portrait of Clarissa Larned that hangs in what is now the periodical room. As a pamphlet from 1906 explains: "It was in the spring of 1900, at the annual April meeting, that the purpose of Mr. [Charles] Larned to donate a large sum toward a new library building was first made known to the town." The building was intended as a memorial to his mother, Clarissa.

Clarissa Larned was born on February 9, 1790, in Weathersfield, Vermont. Her maiden name was Robinson. In April of 1817 she married Jonas Larned of Oxford, Massachusetts. She died May 4, 1869, in Dudley, Massachusetts. Nothing more seems to be known about her, at least nothing that I could find. Nor can anyone offer any theories as to why she haunts the library—if indeed it is her ghost who stalks the stairway. Her bed is one of the artifacts contained in the museum portion of the library in the basement. Does the explanation lie there? [Sorry. I couldn't resist the pun.]

On a more serious note, it should be pointed out that there seem to be at least two, if not more, ghosts haunting the Oxford Library. On several occasions both female and male voices have been heard. Actual sightings, however, have been only of a female figure, presumably Clarissa.

One fascinating aspect of the paranormal goings-on is the large

Clarissa Larned

number of people who have had at least one experience.

Kasia, who started working at the library two years ago, had always heard about the hauntings. Her encounter with the ghost, however, was second-hand. She was upstairs in the new children's room observing a little girl climbing and playing on the slide. Suddenly the child stopped playing. Staring at the base of the slide, she said: "Mommy, I'm scared. There's a ghost over there." She then resumed playing as if nothing had happened.

Sometimes Kasia puts books away, leaves, and returns to find them on the floor.

Susan, a former employee, recalls the security detectors—the alarms that beep if someone walks through with a book that hasn't been checked out at the desk—suddenly going off for no reason. The detector that went off most frequently was the one near the top of the stairway—where Joshua saw "the lady in the picture."

Many employees, alone in the library, have heard the loose floorboard upstairs creak, as if someone stepped on it.

Recently, the carpets in the building were replaced. To complete the job without unduly disrupting the library routine, the flooring crews worked around the clock. In the middle of the night the lights in the building suddenly began flashing on and off. This happened even as the startled workers stared at the light switches—which were not moving.

Although Scott, the custodian who often performs his duties while alone at night, has not actually seen any ghosts, he has had a number of harrowing experiences. As previously mentioned, he frequently hears voices. And the floorboard, upstairs, creaking.

"There have been numerous disturbances ever since the new addition was put on," he told us. (I should state that Scott comes across as intelligent and well educated. As indeed does everyone we interviewed that day.)

A year and a half ago, he told us, he was working alone in the library, carrying a box backwards down the stairway. Although it was mid summer and the weather was seasonably warm, the air in the stairwell suddenly grew cold. At the same moment he felt a sharp pain in his back as if someone had dealt him a severe blow.

"It wasn't just a regular back pain," he said. "It was as if someone deliberately jabbed me with a broomstick. I said, 'Hello, Clarissa,' and the cold immediately went away."

The incident happened in the very same spot where little Joshua sometimes sees "the ghost lady."

More disturbing, though, was something that happened on another occasion around midnight. Scott went upstairs to perform some chore. When he came back downstairs he found that three chairs had been arranged in a semicircle facing Clarissa's portrait.

"I went home early that night," he remarked, dryly.

Intriguing…mysterious…disturbing…weird. These are only a few of the adjectives that came to mind as I listened to Scott's account of the hauntings he's encountered in the last few years. But *spooky…eerie…uncanny*: these and even stronger words are required to describe the sensations evoked by what I can only describe, melodramatically, as Scott's *pièce de résistance*: a tape recording which he played as the three of us sat around a table in a small room in the library's older section, normally reserved for quiet study, that is equidistant between Clarissa's portrait and her favorite spot on the stairway. Had her ghost suddenly shown itself I don't think I could have been more surprised than by what I heard on that tape.

I suppose I'm getting ahead of myself, and should take time to explain the tape's history. In the fall of 2002 Cheryl's son made the recording as a project for his high school psychology class. Essentially, a tape recorder was left playing all night upstairs in the empty library. Scott of course secured the library upon leaving and can attest to the fact that neither the tape nor the recorder was meddled with during the approximately eight hours in which the experiment took place. The eight hours have been condensed into roughly twenty minutes—the interesting parts.

Once again I have to resort to the old cliché of "shivers running up and down my spine" to adequately describe the effect listening to the tape had on me.

I listened to the tape only once. Scott offered to play it a second time, and even offered to give me and Yolanda a copy, but we declined. Once was enough!

This is what we heard on the tape, not necessarily in this order: a sudden, jarring chord being struck on the library piano; footsteps, possibly on the stairway; thumping sounds, such as books tumbling from a shelf might make (the next morning when the library was opened about a dozen books were found to have fallen from a shelf); and voices. Spectral voices.

There seem to be two voices, one apparently male, the other female. The words they speak are unintelligible, and yet, albeit eerie, they are unmistakably voices. They occur more than once on the tape.

Scott says that the tape has been scientifically examined and authenticated. It created a sensation at the high school and indeed throughout the entire town. In Scott's words, "It makes the hair on the back of your neck stand up."

Of course, there's always the possibility that the tape is a fake. But I doubt it. In the first place, there have been and still are weird, unexplainable things happening in the library, not only at night but also in broad daylight. These happenings—which include the sightings of at least one ghost—have been witnessed by a number of people. The sounds on the tape seem to merely bear out the authenticity of these happenings. In the second place, if the tape is a fake, it's a damned good one. Whoever produced it should consider a career in Hollywood. And if a hoax were perpetrated by high school kids, wouldn't the secret by now be out?

These are just thoughts on my part, meant to forestall any doubts those who have not heard the tape might feel by merely reading about it. In any case, there's no doubt in my mind that the Oxford Public Library is haunted. You won't find *me* spending a night there alone.◊

THE HAUNTINGS OF PACHAUG FOREST

A week or two before Halloween, in the year 2004, I gave a talk in Connecticut at the Voluntown Public Library on the subject of "Ghosts, Witches, and Poltergeists." After the talk the library's director, Deborah Fleet, presented me with a copy of a chapbook by a local writer named David Trifilo. I was quite taken by "The Hauntings of Pachaug Forest" and immediately wrote to Mr. Trifilo seeking permission to include the stories in his chapbook as a special section in The Haunted Violin. Mr. Trifilo graciously agreed to my request, and it is now my privilege to share his wonderful stories with the larger audience they deserve.

The Introduction and the four stories that follow are in David Trifilo's own words.

Introduction

The Pachaug Forest is not just any forest. It is an authentic ghost town. Just like the west has their ghost towns, we here in Voluntown have our own. You see, the forest was once inhabited by hundreds of people. They came in the late 1600's and early 1700's and left toward the end of the Great Depression (1929-1939). The Federal Government bought the land back from the landowners who couldn't afford to pay their taxes. All the homes were left to rot away, and now Pachaug Forest stands atop their ruins and conceals the secrets of a very haunted past.

What we must remember when we drive through Pachaug Forest is that we are in fact driving through an ancient village. If you look carefully into the woods, you'll notice the ancient stone foundations of houses and the specifically built rock walls, which were used to hold flocks of sheep and herds of cattle. You can even go right up to the foundations and see stone steps leading into the basements and stand on the very door stoops used by the settlers of Voluntown hundreds of years ago.

Pachaug is indeed a haunted place. Some places are not so frightening, while others will make the hairs stand up on the back of your neck, especially if you cross paths with one of the spirits which dwell in the heart of Pachaug Forest.

The following stories are based on actual accounts reported through the centuries. There are many legends concerning Pachaug Forest. These are just a few I happened to come across in my studies. I'm sure there are many more.

Because of Pachaug's interesting condition and because of its many incontestable ghost sightings, it is considered one of America's most haunted places. Just think, the only vampire in the world that science can't disprove was found on the Geer farm in Griswold just a few years ago! It was a popular story that the Discovery Channel did a special on. That's a fact. And consider the legend of Maude's Grave off of Hell Hollow Road. Maude's ghost has been appearing for the last hundred years on Hell Hollow Road. These are just the well-know stories; the ones in this book are not well known, but are well documented in Voluntown's history, and I intend to make them as well known as the others.

Enjoy...

David Trifilo

Mrs. Gorton's Lilacs

Legend has it that the lilacs around the old Gorton homestead are still prized by the long dead Mrs. Gorton. I heard about this legend many, many years ago and dismissed it for just that—a legend and nothing more. Well, I decided this year to go check it out for myself. I acquired a map of the Pachaug Forest from the Voluntown Town Hall dated 1869. The legend of Mrs. Gorton's Lilacs comes from that period, so I easily found her home on the now decrepit Bailey Pond Road. Today it is nothing more than a foundation; the home has decayed over the last century.

Although Mother Earth has since taken the home back, Mrs. Gorton's lilacs remain. They aren't as proud as they likely once were, but they're there nonetheless, ancient and twisted as they are. Just the fact that they are still there was enough to send chills up my spine.

The legend says that she loved her lilacs so much that she threatened death on any person who stole a bough of flowers from her trees. Her sentiments were well known in the town of Voluntown, and she was thought to be a little insane for the protection of her lilacs. Well, a trouble-seeking fifteen-year-old boy by the name of Jacob Myers decided that Mrs. Gorton's threat was nothing more than a challenge of his nerve. He figured a bough of old lady Gorton's lilacs would be a great trophy to parade around town, so he snuck up in the middle of the night and snipped one and took it home.

The next morning when Mrs. Gorton went outside to care for her lilacs she quickly noticed that a bough of her precious lilacs had been sloppily lopped off. She was madder than a raging bull and decided to go to town to find out who stole her lilacs.

When she got into town she immediately noticed a group of children huddled and laughing at something. She snuck up as close as she could get without being noticed to see if they had her precious lilacs. Sure enough, there was Jacob Myers telling his triumphant story of midnight lilac robbery. Mrs. Gorton charged the group fiercely and grabbed Jacob by his collar and shook him so violently that he let go of the lilacs.

She screamed at him. "How dare you steal from my trees!"

Jacob stuttered and said: "I-I-I didn't, Mrs. Gorton! I didn't steal anything from you!"

"We'll see, young thief," she said as she reached down —Jacob still in hand—to get the fallen lilacs. She raised the lilacs up between her face and Jacob's and studied the lilacs. She looked at Jacob again. "These look like my lilacs, boy," she said loudly. Then she smelled them and growled: "These ARE my lilacs, boy!"

Without saying another word Mrs. Gorton dropped Jacob and walked away with her lilacs toward her home. She acted as if nothing happened. This scared the boys more than being jostled by her, for they knew well her threats of death upon anyone who picked her lilacs.

Many months passed with not even a whisper from old Mrs. Gorton. The month was now October, and Jacob began to visit the ponds behind Mrs. Gorton's house again as he had done regularly before the incident. I guess he figured that she had forgotten what he did.

She hadn't.

No one knows what happened to Jacob Myers on that October day. They just know that he was out by the pond situated just west of Mrs. Gorton's house fishing. The search party found his fishing pole on the bank of the pond, but no trace of young Jacob. The state investigators visited Mrs. Gorton, but felt that she had nothing to do with it, regardless of the stories the townspeople kept telling about her threats.

The case remains unsolved to this very day. The people of Voluntown thought that she buried Jacob between her lilac trees. Passersby in those days mentioned a mysterious fresh dirt mound between the lilac trees just to the right of her door stoop, but no one dared take the chance of disturbing her lilacs by digging there.

Even after Mrs. Gorton was dead and her house rotted away to nothing more than an empty stone foundation, people reported glimpsing an old woman grooming her lilacs with tender care at Mrs. Gorton's house. One person even witnessed her walking across the road one spring night in 1925. The witness said that shortly after seeing the woman, a strong scent of lilacs was smelled. The witness, Hank Farnell, was from Massachusetts and had never heard the legend.

If you'd like to go visit Mrs. Gorton you still can. Her house is on Bailey Pond Road. Go north on Shetucket Turnpike. You'll come to a T in the road. Go left and follow this ancient dirt road until you come to a Y in the road. Stay right. (Left goes to the pond where Jacob disappeared; it's now a swamp.) You'll pass by an open area with a huge mound of sand on your right…You're almost there. Keep going until you see a strange mound in the woods just off the road to your left. This is Mrs. Gorton's house.

If you know what lilacs are, you'll see her lilacs everywhere. When I visited her, I thought it best not to touch her beloved lilacs—you will be wise to do the same.◊

The Breakneck Hill Guard

This is the story of a ghost that appears randomly on Breakneck Hill Road, leading into the heart of the Pachaug Forest. I can't tell you much of the origins of this spirit, but I can tell you he's there, and I can tell you he's probably a soldier from the Narragansett wars of the late 1600's and early 1700's. I can tell you he's there because *I have seen this ghost with my own eyes!*

The legend of the Breakneck Hill Guard can be traced back to 1742 when the first sighting was reported.

When I first started to get interested in the legends of Pachaug, this was the first one I decided to look into for myself. Of course I didn't believe the accounts of a colonial guard walking back and forth at a bend in Breakneck Hill Road, but I thought this certain night would be a good one to go see for myself. It was a windy overcast evening in early November when I was driving by the entrance to Breakneck Hill Road and made a fateful decision to drive up the road.

Now, there are certain unexplainable things that happen to people. I must say, this is one of them! As I was driving I reached a sharp right turn in the road. As soon as I had completed the turn I saw a man dressed in a tattered colonial soldier's uniform marching from the right side of the road to the left. He was carrying a very long musket over his right shoulder. I slammed on the breaks and the man just vanished right there in the middle of the road.

For many weeks I could not bring myself to tell anyone about what I had seen. I thought everyone would think I was crazy or something, but he's there as sure as the sun rises in the morning. That guard is still doing his job at the bend in Breakneck Hill Road.◊

The Cries of the Indian Woman
(The Naming of Hell Hollow)

It is said that during the Narragansett Indian Wars of the late 1600's in this region, an Indian family consisting of three young boys, a young girl, the mother, and the great warrior father were traversing the wilderness of North Voluntown fleeing a band of English soldiers. The soldiers caught up to the family in the middle of the night as they slept in their camp by the banks of the creek running through Hell Hollow.

They were all killed there, but the woman had escaped the initial attack and slipped quietly into the woods. There she watched the massacre unfold. The soldiers began searching for her and found her by the sounds of her shameless weeping in the wood line. She did not try to run or conceal her cries. She felt that she had nothing left to live for, and so she gave herself away to the soldiers, who quickly did away with her.

When the settlers began to filter into the area a few years later, many reported hearing the whimpering cries of a woman, but could never find the source of the cries. This was such a common occurrence that the settlers never settled in that vicinity. It was considered such a haunted place that they called it Hell Hollow, an obvious deterrent to any settlers who would follow.

Even to this day there are no houses in Hell Hollow. It is a very lonely place strewn with boulders and massive trees. The Indian woman's cries are still heard by passersby at the hour of the massacre. It is a brave soul who makes his way through the gut of Hell Hollow at night, waiting for the unknown hour of her anguish to make itself apparent by her ghostly cries.◊

The Lantern & The Pipe

Some of Pachaug Forest's stories are downright eerie. Take for instance the story of old Mr. Dixon. Mr. Dixon lived on his handsome 120-acre farm situated on the hill south of Hazard Pond in Northeast Voluntown.

Late one evening old Mr. Dixon heard a commotion just outside the house. He sprang up out of bed, grabbed his musket, and bolted for the door to see what was causing the noise. As Mr. Dixon stood in the doorway clad only in his pajamas he sternly yelled, "Who's out there?"

There was no answer to his call. Mr. Dixon's wife joined her husband at the door with a glowing lantern which old Mr. Dixon snatched from her and proceeded outside. He raised the lantern high and squinted his eyes to see if he could see what had made the ruckus. All he saw were the leaves falling from the trees, carried by the chilled night air.

Mrs. Dixon begged her husband to come inside and wait until the morning to investigate. Mr. Dixon did not listen and proceeded further out into the darkness. Mrs. Dixon watched from the door as old Mr. Dixon kept going further and further until nothing was visible but the faint glow of the lantern. As time passed, the breeze picked up and was blowing leaves in such thick clouds that Mr. Dixon's lantern was visible only between gusts.

Mrs. Dixon was worried sick for her husband and she called out, "You get back here now!" As she yelled this the wind stopped entirely. All the swirling winds ceased and the dancing leaves settled to the ground. There was a dead silence, not an owl, nor a cricket was heard. Mrs. Dixon was so frightened by the silence that she slammed the door shut and ran to a window to try to catch a glimpse of her husband's lantern from the safety of the house. Nothing…

Mrs. Dixon became more frightened as the seconds grew to minutes. She did not budge from her window perch.

Suddenly there was a slow knocking at the door. Mrs. Dixon looked out the window at the stoop in front of the door and saw no one. She cried out for her husband. "Is that you? Please don't scare me like this! Please!"

Again, a slow knocking at the door. Mrs. Dixon scurried to a dark corner of the bed opposite the window and pulled the blankets up over her head, allowing only a small hole to see through. She shivered uncontrollably out of fear. The knock came again, slow, deliberate and in repetitions of three.

"Who is there?" she cried.

Knock, knock, knock.

Mrs. Dixon had no musket as her husband took the only one they owned, so she crawled along the floor to the kitchen table and clasped a knife. The kitchen table was situated only a few feet from the door, so she stayed, covered in her blanket under the table clutching the knife with tears streaming down her face. She glanced up at the kitchen window, which was just next to the door, and saw nothing but darkness.

Knock, knock, knock.

"Go away!" she cried. "Go away!" Suddenly the light of the full moon broke free of the clouds and streamed along across the kitchen floor, illuminating Mrs. Dixon cowering under the table.

Knock, knock, knock.

Mrs. Dixon decided that she had to muster the courage to open the door and face the uninvited visitor, or better yet—and more hopefully—foil her husband's cruel attempt at a joke. She cautiously and quietly rose from under the table and took the door handle in her left hand while the right was rigidly holding the kitchen knife at ready for defense. While twisting the door handle she noticed that the moonlight had once again disappeared into the clouds. After a few seconds of readying her resolve, she swung the door open and glared into the dark night, ready to slash anyone who attacked her.

Nothing…

The night was so dark that she could not distinguish any features of her yard. She struggled to focus her sight into the night. Suddenly old Mr. Dixon's lantern lit, not more than a foot from Mrs. Dixon's focusing eyes. She fell back into the kitchen and stared at the lantern, suspended there in front of the door as if being held by a person trying to see inside the house. But there was no person!

Then the lantern advanced into the house and turned toward and approached old Mr. Dixon's favorite chair. Mrs. Dixon got back under the table and stared, paralyzed by fear. The apparition seemed interested in something at Mr. Dixon's chair. After much shuffling through Mr. Dixon's personal effects, a corncob pipe lifted close to the light of the lantern and began to turn as if being inspected. The lantern and pipe made their way back to the door, but suddenly paused.

Mrs. Dixon shut her eyes tightly. Through her shut eyelids she saw the lantern's light slowly lower beneath the table right in front of her. The apparition was looking right at her! She could feel it! Then it was all over. She opened her eyes to see the lantern and the pipe swiftly disappear through the open door, into the still night.

Mrs. Dixon leaned over to get a look into her yard. Nothing was visible. Then the breeze picked up again and the moon appeared. It seemed to her like nothing had happened, as if she had experienced nothing more than a bad dream. She closed the door and stayed right there, awake, under the table with her knife until the sun shone bright the next morning.

Old Mr. Dixon never did come home. He was found lodged at the bottom of the well near the foot of the hill in front of their house. It was discovered that the commotion old Mr. Dixon heard that fateful night was made by the barn door, unlatched and clanging in the cool fall breeze.

The widowed Mrs. Dixon said that the ghost was her deceased husband, returning to get his favorite possession—his pipe—and to bid farewell to his beloved wife. Neither the pipe nor the lantern were ever found. Mrs. Dixon swore that every evening at the hour of his disappearance, she could catch a whiff of her husband's pipe carried by the night breeze to her door step. The phenomenon is reported to this day.◊

From the Archives

*I*n "The Man in the Three-Cornered Hat," I mentioned that I had been drawn to Harpswell, Maine, by legends of The Dead Ship. Although famous in its day—poems and even entire novels have been written about it—the spectral vessel, not seen since 1866, is unknown to many modern readers. Perhaps renewed interest might entice it to come out of mothballs and show itself as of old, before vanishing once again into the mists.

In that spirit I have included, in the pages that follow, the story of the Dead Ship, along with two other forgotten ghosts of Maine.

The Dead Ship of Harpswell
by
Charles M. Skinner
(from *Myths & Legends of Our Own Land*, 1896)

At times the fisher-folk of Maine are startled to see the form of a ship, with gaunt timbers showing through the planks, like lean limbs through rents in a pauper's garb, float shoreward in the sunset. She is a ship of ancient build, with tall masts and sails of majestic spread, all torn; but what is her name, her port, her flag, what harbor she is trying to make, no man can tell, for on her deck no sailor has ever been seen to run up colors or heard to answer a hail. Be it in calm or storm, in-come or ebb of tide, the ship holds her way until she almost touches shore.

There is no creak of spars or whine of cordage, no spray at the bow, no ripple at the stern—no voice, and no figure to utter one. As she nears the rocks she pauses, then, as if impelled by a contrary current, floats rudder foremost off to sea, and vanishes in twilight.

Harpswell is her favorite cruising-ground, and her appearance there sets many heads to shaking, for while it is not inevitable that ill luck follows her visits, it has been seen that burial-boats have sometimes occasion to cross the harbor soon after them, and that they were obliged by wind or tide or current to follow her course on leaving the wharf.◊

Jack Welch's Death Light
by
Charles M. Skinner
(from *Myths & Legends of Our Own Land*, 1896)

Pond Cove, Maine, is haunted by a light that on a certain evening, every summer, rises a mile out at sea, drifts to a spot on shore, then whirls with a buzz and a glare to an old house, where it vanishes. Its first appearance was simultaneous with the departure of Jack Welch, a fisherman. He was seen one evening at work on his boat, but in the morning he was gone, nor has he since shown himself in the flesh.

On the tenth anniversary of this event three fishermen were hurrying up the bay, hoping to reach home before dark, for they dreaded that uncanny light, but a fog came in and it was late before they reached the wharf. As they were tying their boat a channel seemed to open through the mist, and along that path from the deep came a ball of pallid flame with the rush of a meteor.

There was one of the men who cowered at the bottom of the boat with ashen face and shaking limbs, and did not watch the light, even though it shot above his head, played through the rigging, and after a wide sweep went shoreward and settled on his house. Next day one of his comrades called for him, but Tom Wright was gone—gone, his wife said, before the day broke. Like Jack Welch's disappearance, this departure was unexplained, and in time he was given up for dead.

Twenty years had passed, when Wright's presumptive widow was startled by the receipt of a letter in a weak, trembling hand, signed with her husband's name. It was written on his death-bed, in a distant place, and held a confession.

Before their marriage, Jack Welch had been a suitor for her hand, and had been the favored of the two. To remove his rival and prosper in his place, Wright stole upon the other at his work, killed him, took his body to sea, and threw it overboard. Since that time the dead man had pursued him, and he was glad that the end of his days was come.

But, though Tom Wright is no more, his victim's light comes yearly from the sea, above the spot where his body sank, floats to the scene of the murder on the shore, then flits to the house where the assassin lived and for years simulated the content that comes with wedded life.◊

The Owl Tree
by
Charles M. Skinner
(from *Myths & Legends of Our Own Land*, 1896)

One day in October, 1827, Rev. Charles Sharply rode into Alfred, Maine, and held services in the meeting-house. After the sermon he announced that he was going to Waterborough to preach, and that on his circuit he had collected two hundred and seventy dollars to help build a church in that village. Would not his hearers add to that sum? They would and did, and that evening the parson rode away with over three hundred dollars in his saddlebags. He never appeared in Waterborough.

Some of the country people gave tongue to their fear that the possession of the money had made him forget his sacred calling and that he had fled the state.

On the morning after his disappearance, however, Deacon Dickerman appeared in Alfred riding on a horse that was declared to be the minister's, until the tavern hostler affirmed that the minister's horse had a white star on forehead and breast, whereas this horse was all black. The deacon said that he found the horse grazing in his yard at daybreak, and that he would give it to whoever could prove it to be his property. Nobody appeared to demand it, and people soon forgot that it was not his. He extended his business at about that time and prospered; he became a rich man for a little place; though, as his wealth increased, he became morose and averse to company.

One day a rumor went around that a belated traveler had seen a misty thing under "the owl tree" at a turn of the road where owls were hooting, and that it took on a strange likeness to the missing clergyman. Dickerman paled when he heard this story, but he shook his head and muttered of the folly of listening to boy nonsense. Ten years had gone by—during that time the boys had avoided the owl tree after dark—when a clergyman of the neighborhood was hastily summoned to see Mr. Dickerman, who was said to be suffering from overwork. He found the deacon in his house alone, pacing the floor, his dress disordered, his cheek hectic.

"I have not long to live," said he, "nor would I live longer if I could. I am haunted day and night, and there is no peace, no rest for me on earth. They say that Sharply's spirit has appeared at the owl tree. Well, his body lies there. They accused me of taking his horse. It is true. A little black dye on his head and breast was all that was needed to deceive them. Pray for me, for I fear my soul is lost. I killed Sharply."

The clergyman recoiled.

"I killed him," the wretched man went on, "for the money that he had. The devil prospered me with it. In my will I leave two thousand dollars to his widow and five thousand dollars to the church he was collecting for. Will there be mercy for me there? I dare not think it. Go and pray for me."

The clergyman hastened away, but was hardly outside the door when the report of a pistol brought him back. Dickerman lay dead on the floor. Sharply's body was exhumed from the shade of the owl tree, and the spot was never haunted after.◊

Sources and Books Mentioned in the Text

A Bottomless Grave and Other Victorian Tales of Terror, ed. by Hugh Lamb (New York: Dover Publications, Inc., 2001).

Celebration of the Town of Oxford, Massachusetts, July 3, 4, 5, 6, 1913, In Commemoration of the Two Hundredth Anniversary of Its Settlement by the English (Oxford, Massachusetts: privately published, 1913).

Country Inns and Back Roads, North America, 22nd edition by Norman T. Simpson (New York: Harper & Row, 1987).

Deep Meadow Bog by Edward Lodi (Middleborough, Massachusetts: Rock Village Publishing, 1999).

Flintlock and Tomahawk: New England in King Philip's War by Douglas Edward Leach (New York: W.W. Norton & Company, Inc., 1966).

Ghosts I Have Known by Curt Norris (North Attleborough, Massachusetts: Covered Bridge Press, 1998).

Grand Manan: Jewel of the Sea by Judith E. Hill (privately printed, 1996).

The Haunted Omnibus ed. by Alexander Laing (New York: Farrar & Rinehart, Inc., 1937).

The Hauntings of Pachaug Forest by David Trifilo (privately printed, n.d.).

Horse and Buggy Days on Old Cape Cod by Hattie Blossom Fritze (Barnstable, Massachusetts: Great Marshes Press, 1966).

I Believe in Ghosts by Danton Walker (New York: Taplinger Publishing Co., Inc., 1969. A re-edited version of *Spooks Deluxe*, 1956).

An Intimate History of New Brunswick by Stuart Trueman (Toronto: McClelland and Stewart, 1970).

Maine Ghosts and Legends by Thomas A. Verde (Camden, Maine: Down East Books, 1989).

More Maritime Mysteries: everyone has a story by Bill Jessome (Halifax, Nova Scotia: Nimbus Publishers Limited, 2001).

Mysterious New England, compiled by the editors of *Yankee Magazine* (Dublin, New Hampshire: Yankee Incorporated, 1971).

Myths & Legends of Our Own Land (Volumes One and Two) by Charles M. Skinner (Philadelphia: J.B. Lippincott Company, 1896).

New Brunswick Ghosts! Demons!...and things that go bump in the Night by Dorothy Dearborn (Saint John, New Brunswick: Neptune Publishing Company Ltd., 1994).

New England Legends and Folklore by Samuel Adams Drake (Boston: Roberts Brothers, 1884).

New England's Ghostly Haunts by Robert Ellis Cahill (Peabody, Massachusetts: Chandler-Smith Publishing House, Inc., 1983).

The Old Colony Town and the Ambit of Buzzards Bay by William Root Bliss (Boston: Houghton, Mifflin and Company, 1893).

Oxford's Two Hundred and Seventy-Fifth History Memory Book: 1713-1988 (Oxford, Massachusetts: privately published by the Historical Commission, 1988).

A Pilgrim Returns to Cape Cod by Edward Rowe Snow (Boston, Massachusetts: The Yankee Publishing Company, 1946).

The Roots of Coincidence by Arthur Koestler (New York: Random House, 1972).

The Return of the Gray Man by Julian Stevenson Bolick (Clinton, South Carolina: Jacobs Brothers, 1961).

A Summer Cruise on the Coast of New England by Robert Carter (1858).

Souvenir of the Charles Larned Memorial and the Free Public Library (Boston: privately printed, 1906).

Tall Tales & Curious Happenings from New Brunswick's Giant Storyteller by David Goss (Halifax, Nova Scotia: Nimbus Publishers Limited, 2002).

Things That Go Bump in the Night by Louis C. Jones (New York: Hill and Wang, 1959).

Virginia Ghosts by Marguerite DuPont Lee (Berryville, Virginia: Virginia Book Company, 1966).

About the Author

Edward Lodi knows his ghosts well. Among his previous books are two collections of true New England hauntings, *Haunters of the Dusk* and *The Haunted Pram*; a book of fact and folklore, *Witches of Plymouth County*; two collections of horror that draw for inspiration upon the grimmer aspects of New England, *Shapes That Haunt New England* and *Cranberry Gothic*; and a fantasy novel, *Witches and Widdershins*. He also edited the acclaimed short-story anthology, *The Ghost in the Gazebo*.

He lives in southeastern Massachusetts with his wife, Yolanda, the famous cookbook author.